Amish Baby Mystery

Ettie Smith Amish Mysteries Book 6

Samantha Price

Copyright © 2016 Samantha Price
All Rights Reserved

ISBN 978-1534656307

No part of this publication may be reproduced, distributed, or transmitted in any form or by any means, including photocopying, recording, or other electronic or mechanical methods, without the prior written permission of the publisher.

Scripture quotations from The Authorized (King James) Version. Rights in the Authorized Version in the United Kingdom are vested in the Crown. Reproduced by permission of the Crown's patentee, Cambridge University Press.

This is a work of fiction. Any names or characters, businesses or places, events or incidents, are fictitious. Any resemblance to actual persons, living or dead, or actual events is purely coincidental.

Chapter 1

"It looks like the rain's going to hold off this morning. Are you going to take Snowy for a walk now?"

From her chair, Elsa-May squinted toward the window in the living room, and then looked up at Ettie who was hovering over her holding Snowy's leash in her hand. "I took him yesterday."

"That walk wasn't very long because it rained, remember?"

"I suppose I should take him, otherwise he'll end up chewing the house to pieces again all day."

Ettie looked down at Snowy who was sleeping at Elsa-May's feet, and then leaned down and clipped the leash onto Snowy's collar before she handed the other end of it to Elsa-May. "There you go." Ettie was keen for a few minutes peace and with both Snowy and Elsa-May out of the house; she'd get exactly that.

Once Elsa-May had taken hold of the leash, she

glared up at Ettie. "Why are you trying to get rid of me? What are you up to?"

Ettie placed her hands on her hips. "I'm not up to anything. There's a break in the rain so you should take him for a walk now. They tell me it's going to rain over the next few days. Who knows when his next walk will be if you don't take him now?"

"Are you sure you're not up to something?"

"What could I possibly be up to? Do you think I'm going to bake a secret pie while you're out? While you're out on your fifteen minute walk?"

Elsa-May sneezed. "Maybe I'm allergic to Snowy. Perhaps I'm getting a cold and should stay inside. You take him for a walk."

"The doctor said that you need to walk—there's nothing wrong with me."

"That's debatable," Elsa-May said under her breath.

Ettie ignored her sister's comment but grew more annoyed. "You'd think of anything to get out of it. Any excuse at all."

"That's not fair to say when I've walked him

nearly every day since we got him, and don't say that I haven't!"

Ettie leaned down and rubbed Snowy's fluffy head while Elsa-May pushed herself to her feet.

"I'll have a pot of hot tea waiting for you and I'll see if I can rustle up something nice for Snowy. Take an umbrella just in case it rains, and take your shawl."

"Ettie, I'm not five years old. I do have a brain in my head to think for myself."

Ettie remained silent as she watched Elsa-May place her black over-bonnet over her white prayer *kapp* and toss her black shawl over her shoulders.

"I'll see you soon, then," Elsa-May said.

"Can't wait," Ettie said under her breath, wondering if she should tell Elsa-May that she'd forgotten the umbrella. Finally she would have fifteen minutes peace, maybe more if the rain held off. Unable to keep the smile from her face, Ettie turned and headed toward the couch.

"Ettie!" Elsa-May screamed after she'd closed the front door.

Thinking that Elsa-May had slipped and fallen on the wet steps, Ettie rushed to the front door and swung it open to see if Elsa-May was okay. On looking closer, she saw Elsa-May was leaning over and looking into a basket.

Thinking that their neighbor had dropped off some more vegetables or fruit for them, Ettie said, "There's no need to scream. You gave me a terrible fright."

Elsa-May straightened up. "Ettie look *inside* the basket, will you?"

The next thing Ettie saw was the very last thing she expected. Ettie stared into the basket to see a small baby fast asleep. "Is that a real *boppli*?" Ettie asked in shock, wondering if it was just one of those lifelike dolls that looked like a baby.

"Help me, Ettie, we must get the *boppli* out of the cold."

Ettie picked up one side of the basket and Elsa-May, with Snowy's leash slipped over her wrist, took hold of the other. They carried the basket into the warmth of the kitchen and placed it on the table.

"Where did the *boppli* come from?" Ettie asked.

"I don't know. He was just there when I opened the door."

"He? How do you know he's a boy?"

"I don't. I just assumed; that's what the *Englischers* do—pink for girls and blue for little boys."

Ettie stared down at the baby, and at the bottom of the Amish baby quilt was a blue blanket.

"Where did you come from?" Ettie asked, peering down at the little baby who, she guessed, was a newborn—not more than a week old.

"I don't know where he came from any more now than the last time you asked me."

Ettie looked across at Elsa-May, wondering what her sister was complaining about now. She wasn't aware that she'd asked Elsa-May anything. "I was talking to him, not you."

"Well, he's asleep so he can't hear you."

Ettie frowned at her sister. "Is he Amish or an *Englisch* woman's baby?"

Elsa-May shrugged her shoulders and then

5

shook her head.

"Well, what will we do? Did someone leave him here because they don't want him?"

"They could've. He's an Amish baby I'm certain of it," Elsa-May said as she studied the baby.

"Whose would he be, then? Why would they have brought him to us? I'd think that if anyone was going to give their *boppli* away, they'd give him to a childless couple or someone who had a large *familye*."

"I think you're right for once, Ettie. It doesn't make sense for someone to bring a baby to a couple of old girls like us."

Unsure of whether her sister had just insulted her or given her a compliment, Ettie decided this was not the time to inquire—much less care. They had to find out why the baby had been abandoned and to whom he belonged.

Elsa-May leaned down and unclipped Snowy's leash. "Off you go, boy," she said before she collapsed onto a kitchen chair.

Ettie sat opposite with the baby on the table between them. "Do we know any young lady who might have been expecting and was trying to hide it?"

Elsa-May's gaze flickered to the ceiling. "I can't think of anyone right away."

"How about a woman who has a lot of *kinner* and doesn't want any more?"

"Humph. Debbie King has too many of them to count. Then there's Becky Fuller who had her eleventh last year. She's put on an enormous amount of weight. No one would ever know whether she was expecting or not."

"That's true, and she looks so pale and worn out all the time. Then there is Sarah Miller who has twelve and she always looks happy, but perhaps an extra would tip the scales in the opposite direction," Ettie said.

They both peeped over the top of the basket at the baby.

"Does he look like a Miller, or a Fuller?" Elsa-May asked.

Ettie shook her head. "He just looks like any other *boppli*. We won't be able to tell until he gets bigger."

"We can't keep him for that long, Ettie."

"We can't give him away either, Elsa-May. Someone left him with us because they knew we'd take good care of him. And do that, we will."

Elsa-May pressed her lips together and narrowed her eyes. "What do you plan to tell people? Will you say Myra suddenly had a *boppli* and left him with us?"

"That's a *gut* idea except Myra is too old to have a *boppli* now." Myra was one of Ettie's daughters who had left the Amish years ago. "They'll take him away and who knows what will happen to the poor little mite. If we call the police, they'll put him in an *Englisch* foster home until they sort things out, and then…"

"We can't be certain he'll be well cared for can we?"

Ettie shook her head.

"Ettie, we must find out who dropped him here

so we can figure out what to do."

After she stood up, Ettie lifted the blue blanket hoping to find some clue to his identity. "There's a note, Elsa-May!"

"Nee!" Elsa-May pushed the chair out and stood up with her eyes bulging. "Why didn't I see that?"

"It was under the quilt—tucked in and hidden by the blanket."

Elsa-May grabbed the note from Ettie's hands and read it aloud. "Please don't let an *Englisher* take my baby. Don't let anyone know you found him or his life will be in danger. Keep him safe!"

"Let me see!" Ettie plucked the note from her sister's hands. After she'd silently read it, she placed it on the table beside the basket.

Both ladies sat back down, stunned.

"Why would his life be in danger?" Ettie asked.

"Someone is hiding him with us. Maybe they don't want us to keep him long-term, they could be hiding him for a short time."

"But who and why?"

"Do you think we should call Detective Kelly?"

Elsa-May asked.

"*Nee*, didn't you read the note?"

"*Jah*, I don't think we should call him either, but I was just seeing what you thought." Elsa-May bit her lip. "What do we do now? We can't keep a *boppli*. People will want to know where he came from."

"We need a plan. We can create a cover story to mask the truth until we figure out what to do. We'll need diapers and baby food, and also clothes."

Elsa-May frowned. "He won't be on food he's too young."

"Stop arguing with me all the time. You know what I mean. He'll need formula, and bottles—all that."

Elsa-May added, "Also some tiny clothes."

"You stay here with him and I'll go out and get everything he needs. Okay?"

"Hurry, though. I don't know what I'll do if he wakes up and cries and I've got no bottle to give him."

Ettie rose to her feet. "I'm on my way. Don't answer the door to anyone. I have an uncanny feeling about this."

"Me too, Ettie, me too."

Chapter 2

When the taxi brought Ettie back home from the store, she stepped up to the front door and heard the baby's cries. After she placed the bags on the doorstep, she opened the door.

"Ettie, where have you been?"

She picked up the bags, moved through the doorway and kicked the door shut with her heel. "I've only been gone half an hour. I had a lot of things to get. How is he?"

Elsa-May was pacing up and down with the baby who was well and truly awake. "Hungry. That's how he is. Mix up that bottle. I've already got a pot of water boiling on the stove ready to warm the bottle."

While Elsa-May continued to pace up and down with the crying infant, Ettie heated the bottle of formula. After five minutes, she tested it on her wrist.

"Should be all good now, Elsa-May."

"Finally!" Elsa-May said as she walked into the kitchen.

"Go sit on the couch and I'll bring the bottle out."

Elsa-May sat on the couch and Ettie handed her the bottle. She put the bottle in the baby's mouth and he sucked eagerly.

"He looks so hungry. I wonder when he was fed last."

Elsa-May shook her head. "Who would leave a baby on the step like that when it's been raining for days?"

"What if they were watching from a distance until you opened the door?"

"They could've been," Elsa-May said staring at the baby. *"Nee.* I remember I looked around and saw no one."

"I'll look for more clues in the basket." Ettie went back to the kitchen and lifted the blue blanket out of the basket and then studied the quilt. She raced back into the living room with the quilt in hand. "Elsa-May, isn't this one of the quilts from

Bethany's store?"

Elsa-May frowned at the quilt that was one inch from her face. "Hold it further back; I can't see properly." When Ettie held it further away, Elsa-May said, *"Jah,* it is. I sold one when I was working in her store and it was exactly that pattern. I remember because I'd never seen that design before."

"I didn't sell one, but I remember this pattern. Bethany told me that most of her quilts are only available in her store. Except for the well-known patterns that she knows people will ask for."

"I don't think that would be correct. That could've been a sales pitch." Elsa-May gave a chuckle.

"Bethany wouldn't need to give me a sales pitch. She said she has a lady making quilts exclusively for her store. If this is one that her lady sewed, there wouldn't be that many of them around."

"And?"

"We go and ask Bethany how many of this style she's sold."

"That's a long shot, Ettie."

"That's the only shot we've got so far. Other than that, we visit all the women in the community with lots of *kinner* and also all the single women who might be trying to hide a *boppli* that they've had out of wedlock. Do you know how many single women and married women are in the community?"

"That would be time consuming, Ettie, but maybe that's what we might have to do. Besides, anyone could've made that quilt."

"I'm certain it's the same as the exclusive ones made for Bethany's store."

"If you're certain, it's worth talking to Bethany. I can't help feeling that it's somehow wrong for us to hide him here like this." Elsa-May stared down at the baby.

"What choice do we have? The note said that his life was in danger."

"Do you think that's true?"

Ettie nodded. "We have to think it's true because if we don't believe it and we're wrong... I just couldn't see any harm come to the little *bu.*"

"Why don't you phone Detective Crowley and tell him you have a hypothetical question to put to him about what would happen if someone found a baby?"

"I can't do that—he'd guess. He'd ask a lot of difficult questions at the very least."

"He might guess that someone you knew found a baby but he wouldn't know that it was us."

"I suppose you're right. Do you think I should? I know he'll say that the baby would have to be handed in to social services or some temporary care thing the government has arranged. Then, he'd go to a foster home while they try to find the mother."

"Get the notepad out, Ettie."

Ettie walked to the bureau and got out a pen and a notepad. Then she sat on one of the chairs opposite Elsa-May. *"Jah?"*

"Write down what we have to do. First, we have to phone Crowley and see what he has to say. Then we, or you, have to go into town and talk to Bethany about these quilts."

"And?"

"We'll know what we have to do when we find out what Crowley and Bethany have to say."

Ettie sighed. "Okay."

"And meanwhile, we can't let anyone know that we have a *boppli* here—and that means no one."

"Agreed," Ettie said and then added, "Not even Ava when she comes to visit?"

"Ettie, *I'm* not the gossiper."

"Are you saying that I am?"

"Well, you do have a habit of talking to everyone."

"Talking is not gossiping."

Elsa-May raised her eyebrows and then stared down at the baby in her arms. "I think he's finished." With his tongue, the baby pushed the nipple out of his mouth. "Did you see that, Ettie?"

Ettie rose to her feet and then leaned over to stare at the baby. "He's so tiny, Elsa-May. Do you realize that ours were that small once?"

"So long ago."

The baby stared into Elsa-May's face.

"He seems quite taken with you, Elsa-May."

Elsa-May chuckled.

"Well, you've fed him, you've walked him up and down and now you'll have to change his diaper." Ettie giggled.

"That's not fair. I've done all those things so you should take your turn doing something for him."

"I went out and got the formula and the diapers. I got those disposable ones so no one would see the cloth ones on the line."

"You mean so you don't have to wash them?" Elsa-May said.

Ettie giggled. "That was an added benefit. I remember washing diapers out by hand when I first got married, before we had our gas-powered machine. I had to boil the water in the big copper kettle. I'm glad those days are long behind me."

"Me too."

"We can take the diaper changes in turn. You go first and I'll do the next one."

"That sounds fair and while I'm doing that you phone Crowley and see what you can find out."

Ettie pulled her mouth to one side. "I hope this

goes all right."

"Just don't let him get suspicious. If he wants to know why, just tell him you've always wondered what would happen, and if he asks any more questions just get off the phone quickly."

"Easy for you to say. You're not the one doing it."

"Would you rather change the diaper?"

"Okay, I'm going now." Ettie grabbed her shawl before she walked out the door. A cool breeze swept over Ettie, making her shiver as she walked down the road to the shanty that housed the telephone. She knew Crowley's mobile number by heart and she hoped he answered it, rather than having her call divert to his pesky voicemail.

After she put the money in the tin, she picked up the receiver and dialed his number.

"Hello." Crowley answered after two beeps.

"Hello," Ettie replied.

"Yes, hello?"

"Hello, this is Ettie."

"Ettie, it's nice to hear from you. How are you

and Elsa-May?"

"We're fine."

"Are you calling me for a reason? Has someone been murdered?"

"*Nee,* well, not that I know of. I have a question for you and that's why I'm calling."

"I'm out on the golf course and they're waiting for me to take my turn. Can we make this quick?"

"What would happen if someone were to find a baby?"

"A baby? Find one where?"

"Hypocritically, if someone found a baby..."

Crowley cut across her, "Hypothetically?"

Ettie pulled a face. She wouldn't let Elsa-May know she'd used the wrong word. Elsa-May had a much better education, which sometimes made her prideful in Ettie's opinion. "Sorry, that's what I meant. Anyway, what would happen if someone found a baby on their doorstep?"

"They should contact the police right away."

"If they did, what would happen to the baby?"

"It very much depends on the circumstances.

The baby would be in emergency care, most likely in a foster home environment until…"

Ettie heard Crowley talk to people in the background.

He came back. "I'm sorry, Ettie, I need to take my turn; I'm holding everyone up. If this is something we need to discuss, I can come by this evening after the 'nineteenth hole.'"

"No, no it's nothing. Thank you. I didn't mean to hold you up. You go and play your game of golf."

"Okay. Bye, Ettie and say hello to Elsa-May."

"I will. Bye."

Crowley promptly hung up the phone.

It was just as she suspected. Why had Elsa-May made her call Crowley? Ettie walked back home, worrying about the baby and wondering what their next move should be. When she pushed the front door open, she saw Elsa-May walking the baby up and down while holding him close against her chest.

"We can't keep him. You know that, don't you?"

"Of course I know that," Elsa-May snapped.

"What did Crowley have to say?"

"He couldn't talk much; he was in the middle of a game of golf. He said the baby would most likely go into foster care—a foster home just like we thought. But that's not an option. You read the note."

"Did you find anything else in the basket?" Elsa-May asked.

"Nothing. I'll take another look." Ettie walked to the kitchen and looked the basket over carefully. There was nothing else in the basket or mixed up within the blankets. "Nothing here," she called out to Elsa-May. "Did you manage to get the diaper changed all right?"

"I figured it out. It's the first time I've used one of those throwaway ones. I've only ever used the cloth diapers."

"Do you think I should go and talk to Bethany now?" Ettie glanced at the clock to see that it was just before midday.

"*Jah,* we should do everything as soon as we can. Crowley always said the leads grow colder the more time ticks away."

"Okay, I'll heat up some soup for us and then I'll go. We have to keep our strength up."

"Good idea."

"Put him down, Elsa-May, you don't want him to get used to being carried everywhere."

Elsa-May looked down at the baby. "He's asleep now. I'll put him back in his little basket." Elsa-May placed him back in his basket on the kitchen table. "Now my back is aching. I wouldn't have thought such a light baby would make my back ache like this."

"It's the way you were holding him. You were arching your back—that's what made it ache."

"You think so?"

Ettie nodded.

"I'll have to be more careful."

"*Jah,* watch your posture." Ettie took the saucepan out of the cold box and put it back on the stove to heat. The day before, she'd made vegetable and pasta soup. It always tasted better the day after it was made.

Both ladies sat down at the kitchen table while they waited for the food to heat.

"It'd be nice if you could come with me," Ettie said.

"I would, but one of us needs to stay here with the *boppli* and we can't take him with us."

"I know. I can't shake the eerie feeling I got from reading that note."

"Put it out of your mind, Ettie."

"I'll try."

"Now, what are you going to ask Bethany?"

"I'm going to take the quilt with me and ask her if they are exclusive to her store. If not, where else are they sold?"

"And also, who makes them."

"*Jah*, and who makes them. *Gut* idea. Anything else?"

"Play it by ear. See what happens. You'll know what to do."

"*Denke.*" Ettie got up to check the stove when she heard the soup bubbling. "It's ready."

"Good. I'm starving," Elsa-May said.

As Ettie poured the soup into two bowls, she said, "Don't forget the baby would probably eat once every four hours—although I think young ones like him might drink more often. Just feed him whenever he looks hungry."

"Don't worry about me, you just worry about yourself. I look after the baby and you go and find out where he came from."

"So, he's definitely a he?" Ettie asked.

"Yes and also he must be only days old because he still has the stump of the umbilical cord. I put methylated spirits on it to dry it out."

"*Gut,* Elsa-May. That brings back memories. I forgot all about waiting for that thing to dry out and fall off. Now, don't we have to take the baby out into the sun so he gets some sunlight to prevent jaundice?"

"Take him into the light—not direct sunlight."

"*Jah,* that's what I meant."

"He looks a *gut* color, but when he wakes I'll take him out back into the garden after I wrap him up well."

Ettie placed a bowl of soup in front of Elsa-May and sat down to one herself.

Snowy ran inside through the dog door and started pawing at Elsa-May's leg.

"Down, boy, down."

"Do you think he'd like some soup?" Ettie asked.

"It can't hurt him I suppose. Put some in his dog bowl and see if he'll eat it."

Ettie poured a cup of soup into his dog bowl. Snowy took a couple of licks and then vigorously shook his head.

"Seems he's not much of a vegetarian," Ettie said.

"He'll have to wait for dinner tonight to get his meat."

As if hearing Elsa-May's words Snowy ran back out through the dog door where he had a kennel close to the house and under cover, out of the rain.

Chapter 3

It had been weeks since Ettie had been anywhere near Bethany's store. With the quilt tucked under her arm, she entered the store and was pleased to see that Bethany was there, rather than one of her workers. Bethany was busy wrapping a package for a lady who was standing at the counter. Ettie waited until Bethany was free.

Bethany looked over and smiled at her. When she'd finished serving the woman, Bethany said, "Ettie, how are you? It's nice to see you. Are you shopping today?"

"Nee, I've come to see you."

"Do you have time for a cup of tea with me?"

Ettie said, *"Nee,* not today I don't. I'm here to ask you a question."

"Really? Well ask away."

Ettie pulled the baby quilt out of the bag she'd carried it in. "Does this look familiar?"

"Jah. That's one of my baby quilts. Where did

you get it?"

"Is this only available in your store?" Ettie asked, hoping that Bethany would say 'yes.'

"That's one of the designs that Gladys makes for me."

"And does Gladys only make this design of quilt for you?"

"I hope so. That's one of my personal designs. She only works for me now that I've got so busy. She doesn't make them for anybody else. Why do you ask?"

Ettie ignored her question and continued by saying, "Elsa-May and I thought it was one of yours. How many of these would you have sold?"

"I think I've sold about six of that design since the store's been open."

"Only six?"

Bethany nodded. From working in the store briefly months ago, Ettie knew that Bethany collected emails and addresses of people who bought quilts from her. She kept a database on her computer.

"Do you still keep records of all your customers?"

"I do. I have a mailing list of all my customers. Why are you so interested in that particular quilt? If there's something wrong with it I can have it fixed. Did stitching come undone or something? If it did, I would be glad to have it fixed."

Ettie shook her head. "It's fine. So, you *do* have a record of everybody who bought this particular quilt?"

When Bethany nodded again, Ettie felt that she might be able to find the person who bought the quilt and be onto the trail of the person who left the baby on the doorstep.

Bethany put her head to one side. "What is this about, Ettie?"

"The thing is, Bethany, I can't tell you. I need to know who bought this very quilt. Is there a way you can tell me that?"

"When I take my customers details, I always assure them it's confidential."

"I assure you, Bethany, no one will know and it's extremely important. It could even be a matter of life and death."

Bethany frowned. "Can't you tell me?"

Ettie shook her head.

"I wish you could tell me what this was all about."

"I'll tell you as soon as I can, but right now—I can't."

"Oh, Ettie, this is putting me in a difficult position." Bethany walked over to her computer and pushed some buttons. "I don't know exactly who bought that very design. I enter people's data according to the money they've spent on a specific item. So I can enter the exact price of that baby quilt, and give you the names of all the people who have bought that exact size quilt. I haven't sold that many of them."

"That would be a help. *Denke,* Bethany."

"I'll print them out for you, but please, keep this as confidential as you can. I shouldn't be doing this."

"It's for a good cause, Bethany. I'll need you to trust me for a while, and I promise to keep it confidential."

"I do trust you, and that's the only reason I'm about to give you all these people's personal details." Bethany stared at Ettie and Ettie nodded.

"Denke, Bethany."

Bethany spent a couple of minutes on the computer before she pressed a button and then looked up at Ettie. "Done!"

Ettie frowned until she heard the whirr of the printer.

Bethany then pulled the two pages out of the printer and handed them to Ettie. "That's all of them. All my customers who bought this size quilt."

"Bethany, I'm very grateful for this. It means a lot to me, and I'll tell you as soon as I can what it's about."

"Okay, and when you're done with that list would you bring it back here so I can shred it? I don't want the names lying around anywhere."

"I will. Now, who makes the small quilts for you? Did you say Gladys?"

Bethany nodded. "Gladys Timberlake."

"Jah, of course, I know Gladys."

"There's no need to talk to her. She only makes these ones for me and I know that because she wouldn't have time to make them for anyone else. These are my own designs, as I said."

"Denke, Bethany, you've been a great help. And this quilt being so unique is going to help me more than you know."

"How about a cup of tea before you leave, Ettie? You look a bit pale."

"Nee, I'll have to get back to Elsa-May, she's waiting for me."

"Is she alright?"

"Jah, she's alright at the moment, although she did sneeze today and she has a bit of a bad back."

"That's terrible. You'd better go home and look after her."

"I will and I'll be in touch soon."

Ettie hurried out of the store with the pages folded in the middle of the baby quilt. Bethany's comments about her looking pale made her feel squirmy in the tummy—maybe it was just nerves. She walked past a bakery and the smell of the freshly baked bread lured her in. A sultana cake with pink frosting caught her eye. Figuring that she and Elsa-May could do with some sugar, she bought it.

Ettie was being driven home in a taxi when she passed Gladys' house. "Stop!" she called out to the driver from the back seat.

The driver slammed on his brakes and turned around. "This isn't the address you gave me." He glared at her.

Ettie looked at the meter, handed him some money and opened the door. "Can you pick me up from right here in half an hour?"

"I don't know where I'll be in half an hour, lady."

"How about you fetch me in *around* half an hour then—twenty minutes, forty minutes—something like that? Beep the horn when you're outside?"

"Okay."

Ettie got out of the car, hurried to the house, and then knocked on Gladys' door. Had she not driven right past her door, she wouldn't have bothered to stop. She'd ask her outright if she'd ever made quilts for anyone else, or indeed, if she had ever made Bethany's baby-pattern quilt for anybody else. If the answer was 'no,' Ettie would know that there was a definite connection between their baby boy and one of those people on the list Bethany had given her.

The door opened, and Ettie saw the small elderly woman standing in the doorway. Even though Gladys was around the same age as Ettie, Ettie always thought of Gladys as an old lady but never thought of herself as one.

"Ettie, it's been so long since you visited me. Come inside." When Ettie stepped inside, Gladys asked. "Where's Elsa-May?"

"She's home. I'll bring her next time I visit. I won't stay long. I was just going home in the taxi and I thought I would call in and see you." She followed Gladys to a sun-drenched sitting room, while carrying the quilt and the pages from Bethany tucked under her arm, and the string-tied cake box in her hand.

"Have a seat; this is where I sew."

Ettie looked around the room to see fabric all over the place.

"Just make some space."

Ettie moved some material over so she could sit down on the chair next to Gladys. She placed the sultana cake beside her and the quilt on her lap. "My, it's such a lovely room here in the sun."

"Jah, and we haven't had much sun lately, have we?"

"Nee, it's been raining so much. It's good to have some blue sky today."

"I see you have one of my quilts." Gladys pointed to the baby quilt.

"Jah. I was just at Bethany's store and she told me that you make these for her. I told her how lovely I thought it was and Bethany said it's her pattern."

"Bethany wanted a line of exclusive patterns that would be purely sold in her own store and not available anywhere else. I told her that anybody could copy the patterns, but she didn't seem to worry about that."

"So you make these, you only supply them to Bethany's store and don't supply them for anyone else?"

"I work seven days a week... Well, not on Sundays—don't tell the bishop I just said seven days." Gladys laughed. "I work on my sewing nearly every day of the week, since making quilts is what I do best."

"Jah, you do a *wunderbaar* job."

"Denke. Anyway, I enjoy it, and why shouldn't I do what I enjoy doing at my age of life?"

"That's true, we should do whatever we want when we reach our age." Ettie chortled. What Bethany had said was true—Gladys didn't make them for anybody else. "And you made this one?" Ettie pushed it forward.

"I can tell just by looking that I did."

"Have a closer look."

"Jah. Why all the interest in this quilt, Ettie?"

"It's just such a lovely quilt that I wanted to

know more about it and know who made it."

"Didn't Bethany tell you I made it?"

"*Jah,* and that's why I dropped by to see you. I haven't talked to you in some time."

"It's always nice to see you. How is Elsa-May doing?"

"She's doing fine. She has a little dog, which keeps her occupied these days."

"I've toyed with the idea of having another dog, but they're so much trouble to look after."

"That's true, sometimes they are, but they're good company when you're lonely. I never thought I would have another dog after Ginger died, and I suppose I haven't, since Snowy is Elsa-May's dog." Ettie jumped when a car horn sounded. "That'll be my taxi." She was sure she'd only been there for five minutes. "I must go. I'll talk to you again soon."

"Please visit again, I don't get many visitors and I don't get out to many meetings anymore."

Ettie felt a little sad for Gladys living there by herself sewing day in, day out, just so she'd have something to do. Maybe Elsa-May wasn't so hard to live with. "I'll be sure to bring Elsa-May next time. Here, I almost forgot about the cake I brought for you. It's a sultana cake." The least she could do was give Gladys the cake.

Gladys' face brightened up. "Oh, I love cake. *Denke*, Ettie."

Ettie, who was nearly at the front door by this time, gave a giggle. "You're welcome. I better get outside before this taxi drives off without me."

"Bye, Ettie."

Ettie waved while hurrying to the waiting taxi. "Goodbye, Gladys." She opened the door and sat in the back seat. "Was that twenty minutes?" Ettie asked.

"It was ten."

Ettie waited for him to give an explanation, but he didn't, and that was all he said during the whole ride.

When Ettie finally arrived home, she pushed the door open to see Elsa-May sitting on her usual chair, knitting. "Where's the *boppli?*" Ettie asked.

"Still sleeping. You weren't gone that long."

Ettie was relieved that the baby was okay. "I feel like I've been around the world and back again." She sat down and told Elsa-May everything that had happened and what she'd found out, and then she handed Elsa-May the list of names.

"It seems these are mostly *Englishers* and many are from out of town."

"I didn't notice that. I haven't had a chance to look at it properly."

"We need a way to find out about these people on the list, so how can we do that?" Elsa-May asked.

"I suppose I'll have to go to the library tomorrow while you're looking after the *boppli* and see what I can find out about them from the Internet. But they're not going to publicly say that they've had a baby if they're hiding that fact—so what use will that be?"

"I don't know, Ettie, I don't know what we're going to do. But you're right, we can't keep the baby forever. Someone is bound to ask questions about the little fellow."

Chapter 4

After the baby's second feeding of the day, Elsa-May put him back into his basket on the kitchen table. He closed his eyes immediately. Elsa-May and Ettie, both exhausted, went into the living room and sat down and drifted to off to sleep. They were woken by a loud knock on the door.

The two women stared at each other.

"Who could that be?" Elsa-May whispered to Ettie.

"I don't know, but I'm nervous."

Elsa-May pushed herself up from the chair. "I'll answer it." She pushed the door open a crack, just enough for her to see who was there. "Yes, what can I do for you?"

When Ettie heard a male voice answer, she scurried to the window to see who it was. It was an *Englischer*. He was a tall man, untidy, and wearing sneakers and jeans, and a jacket with white and red stripes on the shoulders. His face looked hardened, like she expected a criminal's would.

Then Ettie heard him say, "I'm the father of the baby. My wife told me she left the baby here."

"Yes we did find a baby here this morning, but we handed the baby over to the police."

"You did?" he asked.

Ettie closed her eyes tightly, praying that the man would believe her sister.

Elsa-May continued, "Yes, I called the local police, the ones in Main Street, and then they came out."

Ettie opened her eyes to see the man staring at Elsa-May. Ettie knew Elsa-May would be unhappy with the fact she'd lied, but she was doing it to protect the baby. Elsa-May clearly didn't believe that this man was the father of the baby, and neither did Ettie. This man had to be one of the *Englischers* that the mother had wanted to protect her baby from. Now the baby wouldn't be safe here if the man didn't believe Elsa-May. And even if he did believe her now, he'd soon find out she'd lied to him. Ettie put her fingers in her mouth while she listened some more.

"Do you mind if I use the phone?" he asked in a gruff tone.

"We don't have a phone. We use that one down the street in the shanty. It's not ours, it's our neighbor's, but anyone's welcome to use it if they put the money in the tin."

The man didn't look too happy at Elsa-May's suggestion.

"Don't you have a cell phone?" Elsa-May asked.

"Dead battery," was all that he said as he continued to glare at Elsa-May.

Ettie hoped the man wouldn't force his way inside. She walked back to the kitchen, hoping the baby was still soundly asleep. If the baby woke up and cried just at that moment, the man would surely push Elsa-May aside.

Seeing that the baby was still asleep, Ettie got paper and a pen from the bureau and went back to the window. Sure enough, she saw a black car that had to be his. It was one she'd never seen in their street before. From where she was, she could see most of the plate's characters. She scribbled down the three letters and the numbers she could clearly see, and then added combinations of what the other numbers might be. Hopefully, they wouldn't need to contact Detective Kelly, but if worse came to worst they would have to.

"Was the baby all right?" he asked.

"Yes the baby appeared to be well and healthy. Who brought him here? Was it your wife?"

He nodded his head. "We were having a disagreement and she mistakenly thought I didn't want the baby. She's only young and she thought I'd want her to get rid of the baby, but I didn't say…" He put his hand to his forehead pretending to be upset and fake tears came into his eyes.

"Well, I hope you work everything out with your wife."

"The baby is… what police station did you say?"

"I called the one in Main Street. They should know where he is if you go and see them."

"Thanks. I'll go and get him back. Did you see my wife or did you talk to her at all?"

"No we didn't. We opened the door and saw the baby there, and no one was around."

"We? Do you live here with someone else?"

"Yes, my son. He'll be back soon. He phoned the police and then we both waited for the police inside the house. What is your name?"

The man's top lip curled into a snarl. "If I find out you're lying to me, I'll be back."

Chills ran up and down Ettie's spine on hearing the tone in his voice. She peeped out the window and saw him glaring at Elsa-May.

When Elsa-May had closed and locked the door, she stepped back from the window and took a deep breath in and out. "Quick, Ettie, see which car he gets into."

"I've already written most of the license plate number down." As the car drove forward, Ettie was able to see the last two digits clearly. "Got it!" she said. "What should we do now, Elsa-May?

"I must say, that man frightened me."

"Me too, and if he comes back again for the baby what will we do? We'll be no match for him especially if he brings a couple of his friends."

"Do you think he knew I was lying about the baby?"

"Possibly, if he was watching when the baby was dropped outside the house. Come to think of it, if he knew, he could've pushed you out of the way and taken him. He didn't call the baby 'him' or 'her,' I noticed that. I also noticed that he was pretending to be nice to start with then he turned nasty."

"When he didn't get what he wanted he got mean."

Right then there was another knock on the door.

Ettie jumped, and put a hand over her fast-beating heart. "He's back."

"Look out the window to see. If it's him, I won't open the door again."

Ettie took a few steps and looked out the window. "It's Crowley."

Elsa-May opened the door and grabbed Crowley by the sleeve, pulled him inside, and shut the door behind him.

"What's going on?" He stared at Elsa-May with his hands on his hips and then caught sight of Ettie at the window.

Ettie put the notepad and pen down on a low table.

"We should tell him, Ettie."

Shaking her head, Ettie said, "What about the note?"

"We can't worry about the note."

"What about the man?" Ettie said.

"None of us is safe."

"The note must be referring to that very man."

Crowley folded his arms across his chest, looking from one to the other as though he were at a tennis match. "Just tell me what's going on," he demanded.

"What if we tell him, Ettie, but ask him to keep it quiet? He can give us his word."

"Good idea," Ettie looked at Crowley. "Come and have a seat and we'll tell you what's happened."

"I cut my game short. My new friends are cross with me so that's the least you can do." He sat on a chair across from the elderly sisters.

Chapter 5

The sisters told Crowley the whole story: about finding the baby boy at their door, about the quilt, and the list of names Ettie had gotten from Bethany, and the old lady Ettie had visited. They ended their story with the man who'd just knocked on their door.

"I got his plate number."

"Good; we're going to need that. Who has the baby now?" he asked.

"He's in the kitchen," Ettie said.

"He's quite well and healthy. We've been feeding him and looking after him. We've got great-grandchildren; we know what we're doing," Elsa- May said.

"I've got no doubt that you both know how to look after babies, but there's a certain process that needs to be put into place when a baby is abandoned."

"Show him the note, Ettie."

Ettie went to the kitchen and brought back the note and handed it to Crowley.

"It just says not to give the baby to *Englischers* and some rubbish about his life being in danger. Once someone abandons a baby, they shouldn't have any say in what happens—in my book. The law has a different view. A search will begin for the mother and once she's located, she'll receive counseling, and the idea will be to put the baby back into her care."

"I don't think it's the fact that she doesn't like *Englischers.* She said the baby was in danger. It seems that the baby *is* in some danger, and probably from that man who came to the door."

"He said he was the father—what makes you think he isn't?" Crowley asked.

Ettie and Elsa-May looked at each other.

"How would he have known the baby was here?" Ettie said. "And he kept saying 'the baby' rather than 'he' or 'she.'"

"You're making a mountain out of this whole thing. I think that he must've followed the mother and saw her drop the baby here early this morning, and then he's come back to get him. He's probably still watching the house right now. Give me that plate number, Ettie, I'll get an ID on the owner of the car."

"Unofficially, I hope?" Elsa-May asked.

He shook his head. "I'm sorry. I'm going to have to call this in. It's not just about the baby it's about the mother and the father. It's something that affects more than one person."

"But we only told you because we trusted you, and you said you'd keep it quiet."

"I didn't know it would involve an abandoned baby. This is much bigger than both of you realize."

"All we care about is protecting the baby and following the mother's wishes, or the wishes of whoever dropped the baby here. I can feel from the letter that the person was afraid for the baby, and that man was scary. Maybe the mother is in danger, too."

On hearing Elsa-May's words, Ettie knew she was right. This wasn't an Amish baby as they'd first thought. This was an *Englisch* baby who was in danger and someone thought the baby would be safe, hidden, amongst the Amish. Now they'd ruined everything by trusting Crowley—an *Englischer.*

"We have psychiatrists in the Police Force. They'll be able to determine things from the note, Elsa-May."

Elsa-May's lips turned down at the corners. "Detective Crowley, I have years of experience with people—mothers, fathers, daughters, grandchildren. and great-grandchildren, so I think I would know better than some twenty-five year old who's had his head stuck in a book for four years doing some useless degree."

"I'm not a detective now. You can call me Ronald, as I keep telling you both."

"You'll always be Detective Crowley to us," Ettie said.

Crowley smiled at Ettie, and then turned to Elsa-May. "I agree with you, some of the people the department uses might be young, but they do know what they're doing."

"Can you just give us three days before you report this?" Elsa-May asked.

He shook his head. "The first twenty four hours is the most important."

"You can help us find out things without reporting it. We can all do this together while keeping the baby safe. Will you help us?" Ettie asked.

"Twenty four hours," he said. "And only if I help." He shook his head. "I shouldn't let you talk me into this."

Elsa-May and Ettie exchanged glances, and then Elsa-May said, "Forty eight hours? And then we'll tell the police everything they want to know, and we'll hand the baby over. Agreed?"

Ettie was disappointed that they'd be betraying whoever wrote that note. The pressure was on; they had to find out who was out to harm the baby. They had to track down the mother, the real father, or whomever it was who wrote the note and left the baby with them.

Crowley leaned over to shake Elsa-May's hand.

"Agreed. Forty-eight hours, and we'll do this ourselves. After that, you hand the baby in and keep my name out of things the best you can."

"Thank you," Ettie said, knowing that they could all be in big trouble if this blew up in their faces.

"I can get information without letting the force know. I can find out whose name the car is registered in."

"You can do that?" Elsa-May asked.

He nodded. "I still have friends in the force."

"That would be wonderful," Elsa-May said.

Crowley took the slip of paper that had the plate number, and said, "I'll just go outside and make that call."

Once he was outside, Ettie looked out the window to make sure no one was watching them. When she saw that there was no black car in sight, she relaxed a little. It didn't seem as though anyone was watching them or the house, but they still could've been.

Crowley stepped back inside. "They're just running the plates. I should get a call back within the next half hour."

Ettie handed him a list of names.

"What's this?" he asked.

"The names I told you about that I got from Bethany's quilt store earlier today."

He looked down at the names and then looked back up at them in surprise.

Elsa-May said, "What is it, Detective… Ronald?"

"I know this name." He tapped heavily on the paper and then looked up at the elderly ladies once again. "Genevieve Cohen."

"Who is she?" Ettie and Elsa-May asked at the same time.

"Around four years ago, this woman had her baby boy kidnapped and held for ransom."

Ettie and Elsa-May's eyes grew wide.

"What happened?" Elsa-May asked.

He shook his head. "It wasn't my case, but I remember it well. They didn't get the baby back and no one knows what happened to him. The kidnappers asked for $200,000 in cash and gave the parents three days to raise the funds. Of course, the kidnappers told the Cohens not to involve the police. Genevieve was very much against her husband involving the police, but he thought it was the best way to get the baby back. He raised the money, and we had a police officer tail him to the drop the kidnappers had named, and another officer waited near the drop. You see, Cohen had been instructed to give them the money, and a day later, he was supposed to get a call telling him where to collect the baby."

"What happened?" Ettie asked.

"No one turned up to collect the money, and that night, Craig Cohen got a call saying that they'd give him one more chance and if he involved the police again, the they'd kill the baby."

"Did the police stay away?" Ettie asked, doubting that they did.

He shook his head. "By this time, the FBI was involved. At the second drop, the money was collected and the kidnapper caught red-handed. Then the FBI discovered this man wasn't one of the kidnappers, just a petty criminal that they'd paid $500 to pick up the package. The man knew nothing, and his story checked out. The kidnappers never got the money, but the Cohens never got their baby back either. They never heard from the kidnappers again, and our investigations, along with the FBI's, never turned up anything.

"What happened to the baby?" Ettie asked.

"Most kidnapped cases don't end well. They never saw their baby again."

"Crowley, you can't tell the police anything; it might happen again. Do you think that this is that same woman's baby?"

Ettie answered before Crowley had a chance. "I'd say without a doubt it's the Cohens' baby. That's why they're hiding him; they don't want harm to come to this one."

"It's a huge jump to think that, Ettie. Just because Mrs. Cohen bought a quilt at the quilt store doesn't mean that this is her baby. She might have bought it for some other reason. To give away to someone as a present, for example."

"I think I'm right, though. It's a bit much of

a coincidence don't you think? Sounds like the woman—Genevieve—had another baby and she's scared out of her wits that her second baby will be kidnapped. To keep him safe, she dropped him on our doorstep and begged us never to let *Englischers* have him."

Elsa-May said, "I think Ettie's right. Genevieve is hoping we keep the baby within the Amish community."

Crowley heaved a sigh. "Yes, but why the both of you, and why your doorstep? Do you know this woman, have you ever even met this woman?"

Ettie and Elsa-May looked at each other and then shook their heads.

"No, we don't think so," Ettie admitted.

"Then I'd say there's little chance that this woman has left a baby at your door. I'd think if she ever had another baby that she'd keep a close eye on him—not give him away. What you're both saying just doesn't make any sense whatsoever, when you think it through."

"But you will help us anyway?"

"I said I would. We'll have to hurry and plan what we're going to do. Time is of the essence. Now, I always think better with coffee and cake," Crowley said.

Elsa-May pushed herself to her feet. "Coming right up."

Chapter 6

Just as Crowley finished the last portion of his cake, his cell phone rang. He pulled it out of his pocket and looked at the screen. "Ah, it's the station. I'll take it outside." The retired detective bounded to his feet and before he was outside, he answered the phone. "Crowley here." He closed the front door behind him.

Ettie and Elsa-May looked at each other.

"Do you think we did the right thing involving Crowley?" Ettie asked her sister.

"I think we had to, since that man came here looking for the baby."

"I suppose you're right."

Detective Crowley came back inside. "Okay, I found out the name of the man that was here today—Victor Lemonis. He's a petty criminal and he's been in and out of jail since he was sixteen. I'm waiting on my friend to send me a picture." When his cell phone sounded he looked at it, and then showed the man's image to Elsa-May. "Is this the man?"

"Yes, that's the one who was here today. Do you think he might be the father, or a kidnapper?" Elsa-May asked.

"I think you two were right to doubt he was the father. I found out that he's got several complaints against him for not paying child support. Lemonis has six children already, all with different mothers. I doubt that he'd be chasing a baby he thought was his when he's not even looking after the ones he has."

"Six, to six different mothers?" Ettie raised her eyebrows. "He *has* been busy. He must have some involvement with something crooked, then, because it's clear he's not the father."

"I don't think you ladies are safe here. Is there anywhere else you can stay?"

"Not without people finding out about the baby," Elsa-May said.

"I'll talk to someone and see if I can have a patrol car go past your home every so often." He produced another phone out of his pocket. "This is my personal cell phone that I just use for friends and family. Needless to say, I don't get many calls on it except for my golf buddies. And since I just walked out on the game today, I don't think any of them will be likely to ring me any time soon. If the man comes back again, dial 911."

Elsa-May grabbed the phone. "Thank you."

"Do you know how to use it?" Crowley asked.

Elsa-May looked down at the phone. "Yes, I do." He nodded. "Good."

"What are you going to do now?" Ettie asked Crowley.

"I'm off to see Genevieve Cohen to ask her about the quilt she bought. And see what else I can find out."

"What do you want us to do?" Elsa-May asked.

"Nothing for the moment. I'll be back to let you know what I've found out."

When Crowley left, Ettie and Elsa-May walked into the kitchen while discussing how old the baby might be.

"His head doesn't look misshapen at all," Ettie said. "They have an oval head for a while after birth."

"That might mean he was delivered by caesarean section. How long does the head stay misshapen after birth?"

"I'm not certain, only a day or two I think."

"I don't remember my babies' heads being particularly oval-shaped or anything."

"He seems to be healthy and he's got a good appetite," Ettie said.

"He does."

Ettie stared at the baby's face. His tiny eyelashes and barely-there eyebrows were a wonder to behold. She picked up his blue blanket and peeped under it to see his tiny little hands with their perfect fingernails. "It always fills me with wonder when I see tiny babies like this. How detailed are they?"

"Every *boppli* is a miracle. *Gott's* little miracles."

"I hope this one will have a *gut* and happy life."

"We'll pray that he does," Elsa-May said smiling down at the baby.

"Jah, we will. We'll pray that everything turns out well for him and his whole *familye."*

They were interrupted by yet another knock on the door.

"Quick, Ettie, look out the window and see who that is."

Ettie hurried to the window to see Ava. "It's Ava. What shall we do? It'll be all right if she knows, won't it?"

"We can't risk it, Ettie. The more people who know, the more risk there is to the *boppli."*

"What do we do, then?"

"I'll hide the *boppli* in your room with Snowy, and if he cries, we can say it's Snowy."

"We can't put the dog in with the *boppli*. What if he bites him?"

"He's got so much fur I doubt he'd feel it."

"Nee! The dog might bite the *boppli!"* Ettie hissed.

"Ach! I'll lock Snowy outside, then I'll put the *boppli* in your room and if he makes a sound we can say it's the dog. Does that work?"

"It'll have to work. Quick!"

While Elsa-May pushed Snowy out the back and locked the dog door and then put the *boppli* in Ettie's room, Ettie tried to stall Ava. "I'm coming; I'm just tying my shoelace."

"That's all right, Ettie. Take your time," Ava said behind the locked door.

When Elsa-May breathlessly gave Ettie a nod, Ettie unlocked the door and opened it to their young friend, Ava.

"Come in, Ava. I'm sorry it took me so long to answer the door. I didn't know it was you." Ettie stepped aside to allow Ava in.

"You don't normally lock the door. What's going on?"

"Nothing, nothing at all. I didn't realize it was locked." Ettie nervously pushed some of her stray hairs back under her prayer *kapp*.

Ava walked into the living room just as Elsa-May sat down in her usual chair. "Hello, Elsa-May."

"Nice to see you, Ava. Would you like a cup of hot tea?"

"Nee denke. I just had one. Jeremiah wanted me to drop by and tell you that he's nearly finished with the last couple of your chairs. He's fixed the doweling on both of them, and now the glue is drying in the vice. I'm not certain what that means and I hope I said it correctly."

"That sounds correct," Elsa-May said speaking a little too quickly. "The doweling is the little pieces of wood, usually cylindrical—well I think they're always cylindrical—that hold the pieces of the chair together, and then they're glued together for extra strength and held together in a vice while it's drying."

When Ettie noticed Ava frowning at Elsa-May's prattle, she said, "That was kind of him to fix them for us. Won't you sit down?"

"Jah, I haven't seen either of you for a while. What have you been doing?"

"I went into town this morning to visit Bethany. Seems her store is doing really well."

Elsa-May added, "I've just been at home not doing anything very much—nothing at all. We…

we were having a very uneventful boring day until you showed up."

Ava looked from one sister to the other. "Is something going on?"

"Nee, dear. Why would you say that?" Elsa-May asked, blinking too much.

"It's just that the both of you seem to be tense. I feel like you're covering something up."

Ettie raised her eyebrows. "Tense? Us?" Ettie looked at Elsa-May who shook her head.

"Come on. I know you both well enough to know something's up. So, what is it? Has something happened?"

Right on cue, the baby cried.

Ava frowned. "What's that?"

"It's Snowy. He knows we've got a visitor and he doesn't like being left out especially when the weather is a bit cold like it is today."

"He's a very sociable dog," Ettie added. "He's been crying a lot lately whenever someone comes to visit."

When the baby cried again, Ava asked, "Why

don't you let him in? Snowy's always inside."

"My dog trainer, Quinton, said that it won't hurt him to be outside for a bit every day. He's not a person, he's a dog. He needs to know that he's not the 'top dog'. Dogs are pack animals and they follow a leader. I need to be his leader and I can't do that if he's inside under my feet all day, can I? *Nee!* I can't."

The baby cried again.

"Sounds like a baby." Ava leaped to her feet and started toward the back door and Ettie's bedroom, which was right next to it.

Elsa-May hurried behind her and stood in front of Ettie's bedroom door. "It was nice of you to stop by, Ava, but now Ettie and I are tired and need a nap."

Ettie was sure all was lost but tried to help as well. She hurried toward Ava telling her how tired she was from her trip to town.

Ava folded her arms in front of her and leaned back. "I know there's a *boppli* in there, and by the sounds of the cry it's a newborn. Tell me what's going on and why there's a baby in there."

"We might as well tell her, Elsa-May."

Elsa-May opened Ettie's door and Ava walked in. She stood over the basket. "It *is* a *boppli.*"

"Good guess," Elsa-May said, now glaring at Ettie.

Ettie shrugged. "She guessed; I didn't tell her."

"I was right about you not being able to keep a secret."

"It won't matter if Ava knows."

"She didn't keep that secret from Jeremiah did she?" Elsa-May said shaking her head.

"What secret was that?" Ettie asked.

"When we went over to her house that time when she was asking Jeremiah's friend questions and we were there listening to the answers."

"That's right, but she did keep it secret until Snowy rushed into the living room and gave us away. She didn't want to keep secrets from Jeremiah. Ava felt bad about not telling Jeremiah the truth of the whole thing. You know how straight-laced Jeremiah can be and Ava knows that."

"Hey, I'm right here," Ava said before she looked back at the *boppli*. "I'll keep your secret whatever it is as long as I can hold him."

"You won't tell Jeremiah?"

"Nee, not unless he asks me if you're hiding a *boppli*. If he asks me that, then I'll have to tell him."

"Sounds fair, Elsa-May," Ettie said.

"All right. Pick him up, but mind his head. He's likely only days old."

Ava picked the baby up and rocked him to and fro. "I've been praying for a *boppli*. Does this one have a *mudder* or can I have him?"

Ava was joking, not realizing the baby had been left there.

"I'll heat up a bottle while Ettie tells you the whole story," Elsa-May said.

"She might be able to help us with something, Elsa-May."

"Jah, she could I suppose. As long as she doesn't tell anyone."

"She said she wouldn't," Ettie said.

"Again—I'm right here," Ava said with her face against the baby's.

Chapter 7

Ava sat on the couch giving the baby his bottle while Ettie explained all that had happened.

"That's so scary with the man coming to your door. And he's a criminal you say?"

"That's what Crowley said." Elsa-May nodded. "Crowley got one of his police friends to run his plates through their computer and send him the man's picture, and then he showed me the man's photo on his cell phone. It was the very same man who came to the door."

"And the man said he's coming back if he finds that the baby was not handed over to the authorities."

"The baby's not safe here. That man could come back here any minute," Ava said looking down at the baby.

"He's as safe here as anywhere," Ettie said.

"How can you say that, Ettie? That man could come back any time, force his way in, and take him. You two wouldn't be able to stop him. I'll have Jeremiah come over here to stay with you."

"I told you this would happen, Ettie." Elsa-May glared at Ettie. "Pretty soon the whole community will find out."

Ettie shook her head at Ava. "You said you wouldn't tell anyone."

"Jeremiah won't say anything, and he'll be able to protect the baby and both of you."

"But Crowley only gave us two days. No one will find out in two days. I'd feel much safer if Jeremiah were to stay here for two days—two nights. The man is unlikely to come here if he sees we have a man about the place."

"Ettie's right," Ava said to Elsa-May.

Elsa-May let out a loud groan.

"It will be a good idea to have an extra person about the place," Ettie said.

"Especially a man," Ava added with a smile.

"I suppose that's best for the safety of the *boppli,*" Elsa-May admitted. "Just as well you came over here today, Ava."

"I wasn't going to, but something told me I should come here on my way home and let you know about your chairs."

"Everything works out for the best most often," Ettie said.

"That's what our *vadder* used to say, didn't he Ettie? Now that would've been Jeremiah's great-grandfather. Is that right?"

"Jeremiah's your grandson—*jah*, that's right—his great-grandfather," Ettie said. "Well, don't tell Jeremiah why he's coming over here. Just tell him that we'll tell him everything when he gets here. Okay?" Ettie asked.

"Okay."

"Are you sure he won't mind coming here?" Elsa-May asked.

"Of course he won't mind. He'd do anything for you two. And it'll help him get used to having a *boppli* around." Ava giggled.

"So you have an agenda of your own?" Ettie asked with a twinkle in her eyes.

"I might have."

"Do you want us to show him how to change diapers?" Elsa-May asked.

"Don't bother. He already told me he won't be doing any of that."

Ettie giggled. "We'll see about that."

"Are you going to have him change a diaper?" Ava asked with her eyes widened.

"It won't hurt him to know how to do it," Elsa-May said.

"I suppose you can try to talk him into it."

Elsa-May laughed. "We won't give him a choice about it. That's usually the best way with men."

"Sounds like he's in for a fun time. I'd better get home in time to fix his dinner and let him know he'll be coming here. I'll try to get him to leave home before it's dark."

"Before dark would be good," Ettie said, worried that the man might come back.

"Denke, for coming here, Ava."

"You're welcome, Elsa-May." Ava kissed the baby on top of his head and then stood up cradling him in her arms. "Who wants him?"

Elsa-May stood. "I'll take him."

Both ladies walked Ava to the door.

When she was gone, Ettie said, "Well, we'd better rustle up something for dinner, Elsa-May, you know what an appetite Jeremiah's got. Even though Ava said she'd give him a meal, that man can eat two dinners—no problem."

"I'll take care of the *boppli* while you cook."

"Okay. Shall we give him a name rather than call him 'the *boppli*' all the time?"

"Good idea. He looks like a 'Luke' to me," Elsa-May stated.

"You thought of that pretty quickly. Have you been thinking about a name for him?"

"Nee. I looked at him just when you said it, and then I thought of the name 'Luke.' He looks like a 'Luke,' don't you think?"

"All right, that's as good a name as any. We'll call him Luke," Ettie said before she turned to rustle through the pantry. "I'll need to bake more bread and I'll make an apple pie for dessert."

"What about the main dish?"

"Let's see now." Ettie moved some cans around in the pantry to get to the back. "I can make some cheesy chicken and rice."

"*Gut!* I love that. Why haven't you made that more often?"

"It's a little time consuming, but I'm sure Jeremiah will like it." Ettie knew that she'd gotten the raw end of the deal. With disposable diapers and feeding Luke every couple hours, Elsa-May had taken the easier option. As Ettie brought all the ingredients for the meal out of the cold box, she asked Elsa-May, "When do you think Crowley will come and tell us what Mrs. Cohen said?"

"He should come back here today—that's what he'd said he'd do."

"Would he come here today even if it's later tonight?"

"I'd say so."

Ettie looked at the food and knew she had to make certain she had enough so she could invite Crowley to stay for dinner if he came around the time of the evening meal.

"You'd better make enough dinner for Crowley, too, if he arrives near dinner time."

"Jah, I was just thinking the very same thing. I hope he's found something out. Do you think she might be Luke's *mudder?"*

"I do, but Crowley seems to think it's a long shot."

When Ettie was half an hour into cooking the dinner, a knock sounded on the door. "Elsa May, will you get the door? That should be Jeremiah now." Ettie heard Elsa-May's footsteps head to the door, and seconds later, she heard Jeremiah's voice. Ettie was immediately relieved that it was Jeremiah and not that dreadful man back again. She hoped Elsa-May had looked out the window before she'd opened the door. Surely she would have.

Minutes later, Jeremiah came into the kitchen and gave Ettie a kiss on the cheek. "Hello, Aunty."

She giggled at him calling her 'aunty' when for the past several years he'd dropped the 'aunty' and called her just 'Ettie.' "Hello Jeremiah, *denke* for staying with us. Ava has told you everything, has she?"

"She has, and she told me how important it was that I keep quiet about it."

Elsa-May walked into the kitchen. "See, Ettie, no one can keep their gums from flapping."

"What? I haven't said anything to anyone," Jeremiah said.

"Good!" Elsa-May said, "At least that's someone who's kept their trap shut, but we told Ava that we'd tell you when you got here." She sighed. "I guess I'll need to heat another bottle about now. You should watch and see how it's done, Jeremiah; it'll be your turn soon."

"*Nee* not yet," Ettie said. "It's not quite time yet and I'm using all the burners."

"All of them?"

"*Jah,* this is a complicated dish. I have to make the cheese sauce separately."

"Cheese sauce! Sounds *wunderbaar.* I like anything with cheese in it," Jeremiah said. "You could warm the bottle in hot water, Elsa-May, what about that?"

"That will have to do."

"I won't be long," Ettie said.

"I'll get it all ready to go." While Elsa-May got the formula ready, Jeremiah sat down at the kitchen table.

"*Denke,* for fixing those chairs, Jeremiah. Ettie, Jeremiah just brought back the last of the chairs."

"Those chairs have been needing fixing for ages," Ettie said. "*Denke,* Jeremiah."

"It's nothing. You should've told me much sooner and I would've come and fixed them right away."

"We don't like to bother you," Elsa-May said.

"Where's the *boppli?* Can I see him?" Jeremiah asked.

"We're calling him Luke," Ettie said.

"You're not growing too attached to him, are you?" Jeremiah swiveled in his chair to face Ettie.

"*Nee,* we just thought we should give him a name."

"Can I see him?"

"He's asleep in Ettie's room at the moment. It's the quietest end of the house. He'll be awake soon enough. I don't want to show you now in case he wakes up and there's no warm bottle."

"Tell me more about this man who came to the door."

Elsa-May told him everything that had happened and all about the man who'd come to the door and what Crowley had found out about him.

"He still could've been the father," Jeremiah said.

"Maybe he was," Elsa-May said. "We don't know for certain, but still, we were not going to hand Luke over to anyone."

"If he's a criminal, maybe the mother was trying to keep him away from the baby."

"What about the quilt?" Ettie asked.

"Any number of people could've come by the quilt. It might have been a gift from someone. I guess the detective will have to go through all the names of the people who bought quilts like that and find out what became of them," Jeremiah said.

"That's time consuming, but I suppose that will have to happen if the mother can't be located in any other way," Elsa-May said.

"If that man was the real father you do understand that he will have rights?"

"Jeremiah, we're not trying to keep the baby from the man if he's the real father. We just didn't believe he was."

"I know. I'm just saying..."

"Crowley's been gone a long time. I wonder if he's been talking to that quilt woman all this time," Ettie said.

"Quilt woman?" Jeremiah asked.

"The woman who bought the quilt from Bethany's store, and who had her baby kidnapped four years ago. I thought Ava told you everything."

"Yeah, she did. I get the feeling both of you might be convinced that this baby is hers?"

"That's right. That's what Ettie and I think at this stage, at least until we get more information."

"I sure hope you find the parents of the baby. There will be someone out there missing him already."

"That's what Ettie and I hope. We hope someone is missing him and really wants him. Otherwise, we'll have to find a family who really wants him."

"How about a cup of tea while you're waiting for dinner, Jeremiah?" Ettie asked.

"Are you finished with one of the burners now, Ettie, so I can warm the bottle?"

Jah, I've got a spare one now."

"Can you wait for your tea?" Elsa-May asked Jeremiah.

"Of course I can wait."

"Jah, he can wait because dinner's nearly ready. It's only about fifteen minutes away. Can you wait that long, Jeremiah?"

Jeremiah chuckled. "Of course I can. I had a little bit of something at home before I came here."

Right then the baby cried.

Jeremiah smiled. "Good. I can see him now."

"Come with me," Elsa-May said. "I'll let you pick him up."

Ettie was glad she was alone in the kitchen. She

didn't like people hovering around while she was cooking. Seeing the made-up bottle of formula, she popped it in the waiting saucepan, set the pan on the stove, and turned on the gas.

Elsa-May came back into the kitchen with Jeremiah, who was carrying Luke.

"Luke seems to like Jeremiah. He stopped crying when Jeremiah picked him up."

"Gut! I've got the bottle heating. It shouldn't be too long."

Elsa-May smiled. "I'll set the table, then."

When they heard a knock on the door, Jeremiah said, "Do you want me to answer it?"

"Keep the *boppli* here; I'll see it is who it is first," Ettie said hurrying into the living room. She pulled the curtains back to see Detective Crowley. "It's only Crowley," she yelled out before she opened the door. "Come in," Ettie said to Crowley. Then she noticed that Jeremiah had come up right behind her. "Do you two know each other?" she asked Crowley.

"I don't believe so," Crowley said.

"This is my grandnephew, and Elsa-May's grandson, Jeremiah."

"I think we might have met before," Crowley said.

"Possibly. You're the detective? From the investigation at Agatha's house?" Jeremiah balanced the baby in one arm while he shook Crowley's hand.

"Retired detective," Crowley corrected him, "and yes, that's where we met."

"Did you get to speak to Genevieve?" Ettie asked the detective as Elsa-May came out of the kitchen. "Jeremiah knows everything. He's staying the night to make sure we're safe."

"Good idea. I'm afraid I talked to her, but didn't get very much information."

"Did she admit to being Luke's mother?" Elsa-May asked him.

"We're calling the baby 'Luke.' Have a seat and tell us everything," Ettie said.

"Wait!" Elsa-May said. "I'll just check on that bottle." When Elsa-May came back out of the kitchen, she had the bottle in hand. Then she organized Jeremiah to sit next to Ettie on the couch and feed the baby.

"Okay, we're ready to hear all about it now," Ettie said.

"When I arrived there, I told her I was doing follow-up investigations of her baby that was kidnapped four years ago. She invited me inside and I talked to her, but her husband was at work."

"And what did she say?" Ettie asked.

"More importantly," Elsa-May said, "what did you ask her?"

"I went over some basic facts about the kidnapping. She was hopeful I had some new information. I had to tell her I was a retired detective and that I wasn't there in an official capacity. She didn't mind when I explained that I was doing some work on the case in my own time."

"What did she say about the quilt?" Ettie asked.

"When I asked her about the baby quilt she'd bought, she clammed up. After that, she wouldn't say any more."

"Had she had a baby recently?" Elsa-May asked.

"I asked her that at the beginning of our talk and she said that she hadn't. I did notice that she looked dreadfully nervous."

"Is there any way you could find out if she's had a baby?" Ettie asked.

"I checked into that. There's been no birth registered. Apart from asking her doctor, I don't know any other way to find out. I can't request the information from her doctor without some kind of official backing."

"Don't you have a friend who works at the hospital?" Ettie asked.

"I do, but only in one hospital and she could've had the baby anywhere."

"And maybe not even in a hospital," Jeremiah interjected while he was feeding the baby in his arms.

"The dinner will be ready now," Ettie said, pushing herself out of the chair.

"Will you stay for dinner?" Elsa-May asked Crowley.

"I've made more than enough," Ettie added.

"Are you certain that will be all right?" Crowley asked.

"Of course, we'd love to have you stay for dinner, and I've made dessert."

"I will; thank you. Everything smells delicious. I've always enjoyed your cooking, Ettie."

Over dinner, Crowley told them word-for-word his entire conversation with Genevieve.

"Did she look like she'd had a baby recently?" Ettie asked.

Crowley shrugged. "I wouldn't know. If I was still on the force, I could do a better investigation of all of this, and talk to the husband. She acted very strangely when I mentioned her husband, and I wouldn't be surprised if he held the key to all of this, or held some kind of information."

"Can you have one of your friends look into her credit card information?" Elsa-May asked.

"I'll see what I can do, if I'm not stretching the friendship too much."

"Do your best for us and little Luke," Elsa-May

said leaning forward to the detective.

The detective raised his eyebrows. "Remember our deal? I said I'd give you two days—one already gone."

"You did say you'd help us in those two days. Don't forget that."

"What's this about two days?" Jeremiah asked.

Crowley answered, "I made a deal with these ladies that I would give them two days and after that, I'll have to alert the authorities, if we haven't tracked down the mother by then."

"What about the note that said not to leave the baby with *Englischers?*" Jeremiah asked. "Ava and I could look after the baby until his mother is found."

"That would be good." Elsa-May looked at Crowley. "Would they let Ava and Jeremiah look after the baby?"

Crowley scratched his neck. "It's a possibility, and it could help that there was a note left with the baby with a preference for the baby to stay amongst the Amish. You might need to have a background check run, but they can do those things pretty quickly. They'll also need to come out and take a look at your house, and ask a lot of questions to make sure the baby will be in a safe environment. You could qualify as foster parents."

Ettie put a hand over her heart. "That makes me feel so much better. I do hope we can keep this baby safe."

"I said it's a possibility. It'll be entirely up to social services."

* * *

When Crowley left, Ettie and Elsa-May decided between themselves that Ettie would sleep on the couch and Jeremiah would take her bed. Jeremiah volunteered to wake up for the baby's nightly feedings, saying he'd get used to waking in the middle of the night just in case he became a foster parent. That suited Ettie and Elsa-May just fine.

Once Jeremiah was in bed with the baby in the basket beside him, Elsa-May sat on the edge of the couch while Ettie arranged the blankets over herself.

"Are you going to have enough room?" Elsa-May asked.

"*Jah.* I can fully stretch out. It's just like a bed and just as comfortable. I don't mind sleeping here at all."

Elsa-May breathed out heavily. "You know what we have to do now, don't you?

Ettie sat up straight. "Go to Genevieve and talk with her?"

"Exactly."

"I figured Jeremiah and Ava can look after Luke tomorrow and we know he'll be safe. Genevieve will be much more likely to talk to women about her babies than talking to a man."

"That's exactly what I was thinking. And we'll take the baby quilt with us and see the look on her face when she sees it."

"Good idea, Elsa-May."

"Do you think Jeremiah will mind taking Luke tomorrow?" Elsa-May asked.

"Of course he won't mind and neither will Ava. He was asking about them being foster parents. They're both like a couple of broody hens."

They both giggled quietly so Jeremiah wouldn't hear them.

Chapter 8

Their plan worked and Jeremiah headed off with Luke in his buggy early the next morning. Jeremiah was going to take the day off, so both he and Ava would look after the baby at their house. In case anyone was watching Elsa-May and Ettie's house, Jeremiah had taken Luke to his buggy in a laundry basket.

"Come on Ettie; he's gone now."

"I'm coming, I'm just getting my boots on." While sitting on her bed, Ettie laced up her boots and tied them in double knots. They were off to talk to Genevieve Cohen.

When Ettie came out of the bedroom, she saw Elsa-May brushing Snowy. "He'll have to wait for his walk today until we come back."

"I'm sure he won't mind."

"Do you think we should've let Crowley know we're going to talk with Genevieve?"

"Of course not!" Ettie said. "He would've had

some reason why it wouldn't be a good idea, but the way I see it, we don't have anything to lose. She's the only person with any connection to Luke so far, and even though the detective thinks it's a long shot that she's involved, we need to see her."

Elsa-May nodded and placed Snowy back down on the floor before she pushed herself to her feet. Once she'd thrown the dog brush down on her chair, she looked up at Ettie. "Let's go then."

"Do you know where she lives?" Ettie asked.

"Nee, don't you?"

"How would I know that?"

"Why did you say we should see her, then?"

Ettie shook her head, quite disgusted with Elsa-May. She should've thought this through better. "Elsa-May, do we still have that cell phone that Crowley gave us for emergencies?"

"Jah, we do."

"Let's try to phone Information and see if they'll give us the address."

"Won't they only give a phone number?" Elsa-May asked.

"Then we'll call Genevieve and see if she'll give us her address."

"I doubt she will." Elsa-May said, "We know the general area she lives in and that's a start. Do you remember what her husband's name is?"

"Didn't Crowley say 'Craig' when he mentioned him last night?"

Elsa-May picked up the cell, turned it on, and then dialed the number for Information. "Quick, get me pen and paper."

"It's a good thing you still remember how to use a cellphone. We had one once remember? Until the bishop let on he knew about it and you thought you should get rid of it."

"Shh. It's ringing." Elsa-May got the phone number of the residence and then ended the call. "I think I can get onto the Internet with this phone. I couldn't with my old one." After she had clicked a couple of buttons, she managed to find the Cohens' address, which she wrote down.

"How on earth did you do that, Elsa-May?"

"Well, they don't have much security. They don't

even have an unlisted telephone number."

"That's strange, isn't it?"

"Seems strange to me if they've got a lot of money like Crowley said, and they've had problems before."

"Let's go."

Elsa-May and Ettie hurried down to the end of the road to call for a taxi.

When the taxi dropped them off, they were faced with a house surrounded by a high fence and high metal gates.

Ettie stared up at the gates, hugging the folded baby quilt. "What was that about them not having much security?"

"I guess this is why they aren't too careful about people knowing where they live. How are we going to get through those gates?"

At that moment, a car drove into the driveway, and the driver spoke into the intercom. Two seconds later, the gates were opening and the car was driving through.

"Quick, Ettie."

Before Ettie could think, she was being dragged through the opening gates. Then Elsa-May pulled her behind some bushes when the large double gates began to close.

"Now what do we do?" Ettie asked, crouching down with her long dress brushing the grass.

"We'll see who's in that car." They watched as a lady in a black and white uniform got out of the car.

"It's the maid by the looks of her," Ettie said.

"We'll wait a while, and then we'll knock on the door."

"What if they can see us? There could be cameras around or they could have big attack dogs."

"We like dogs, don't worry about it. You're always looking on the down side of things."

"I'm not. I'm being practical. One of us has to be."

"Stop talking, Ettie. Less talking and more action." Elsa-May stepped out from the hedge and tugged on her sister's sleeve, pulling her up off the grass as Ettie hugged the baby quilt under her other arm. "Let's go."

Ettie stumbled toward Elsa-May and had no choice but to follow as Elsa-May strode confidently on the white pebbles of the driveway toward the front door. Their footsteps crunched underneath them and Ettie was certain the people inside the house must've heard them approaching.

After Elsa-May had pressed the call button, she waited for the tall white double doors to open, while Ettie stood behind her.

To their surprise, a woman spoke to them through an intercom. "Hello?"

"Hello, we need to speak with Mrs. Cohen. Is she available?"

"How did you get in?"

"Through the front. We need to speak with Mrs. Cohen; it's a matter of great importance."

"Who wants to speak to her?"

"She doesn't know us. It's urgent that we speak to her, though."

Ettie leaned forward. "We have some private

information to give her."

"Just a moment," the voice replied.

Elsa-May turned around and raised her eyebrows at Ettie. Then her gaze fell to the quilt under Ettie's arm. "It's *gut* that you remembered that."

"Of course I remembered it."

Right then, the door opened and a woman stepped out. The woman had a pale face and her dark hair was severely drawn back into a bun. Her eyes stood out against her gaunt white face as did her thin lips that were painted blood red. "How did you get in here?"

"We followed a car in," Ettie said.

"Name?"

Elsa-May scratched her neck. "We don't know who it was. It looked like a cleaning lady."

The woman narrowed her eyes. "No! What are *your* names?"

"I see, I thought you meant the name of the woman from the car we followed in… but, of course, you'd probably know who that was."

Ettie thought she'd better interrupt or they'd be

there all day. Taking a step forward, she said, "I'm Ettie Smith and this is my sister, Elsa-May Lutz. Are you Mrs. Cohen?"

"I work for her. What's all this about?" The woman folded her arms across her thin frame.

"Can we see her? We've come a long way and we've got some confidential information for her."

"About what?"

"It's about this." Ettie pulled out the quilt and the woman stared at the quilt and immediately unfolded her arms and straightened up.

"You'd better come inside." She pushed the door open for the ladies to walk through. "You'll meet with her in this room. I'll tell her you're here." Just to the left of the hallway was a sitting room. "Please, have a seat."

They were only in the room for two minutes before another lady walked in. "Hello," she said.

Ettie and Elsa-May stood and introduced themselves.

"Have a seat," Mrs. Cohen said as she sat down. "You're here about the quilt?" she said as her eyes went right to it.

Ettie began, and got to the point. "You left your baby at our door, didn't you?"

She opened her mouth to speak, then looked from Ettie to Elsa-May as though she were searching for words. She sobbed and pulled a lace handkerchief out of the front pocket of her pants. "I did." She looked at them. "Where is he?"

"He's safe with some friends of ours."

"Amish friends?"

Ettie nodded. "Amish friends. Don't worry, he's safe and he's being looked after well."

"Do you think someone is going to steal this baby like they stole your baby five years ago?" Elsa-May asked.

"It was four years ago, and it's likely. We never got our Langley back. I can't go through that again. Did you know that a detective was here? They were no help last time and I wish they'd just stay away."

"He's a retired detective—a friend of ours— he just wants your baby to be safe the same as Ettie and I do."

"Will you tell us what happened with Langley?"

"He's dead."

"Presumed to be? I thought they never found him," Elsa-May said.

"They told me that's what happens when kidnappers don't get their money. My husband, Craig, was speaking to the people who took our baby, he'd agreed to give them the money. He stupidly got the police involved and they called in the FBI. That's when everything went wrong. Craig arranged to drop the money where they wanted. After Craig took the money there, the police swooped in on the man and we never got the call to collect Langley. I mean, of course, we wouldn't because they never got the money they asked for. Turns out the man they caught was someone they'd hired to pick up the money—he knew nothing about the kidnapping or the men who did it. It was botched all the way along, and I blame the police—and my husband." She shook her head and in a low tone said, "If Craig had just given them the money like they'd asked, I'd be sitting here with Langley today."

"You don't know that for certain, Mrs. Cohen, and you can't live in fear," Elsa-May said.

"I can't risk anything happening to my baby. That's why I gave him away. My husband doesn't even know about the baby. Please don't tell him."

"How is it that he doesn't know?" Ettie asked.

The woman mopped up some more tears before she confessed, "As soon as I found out I was pregnant, I flew to Canada to stay with my sister. I had the baby there and on my way back here, I knew I had to leave him with the Amish. I could have left him in Canada, but I'd feel better knowing he was living close by. I saw…" she turned to Elsa-May. "I think it was you I saw walking a dog. You looked kind and I watched you go into a house. I then left and drove around all night wondering if I was doing the right thing. In the morning, after I'd given him a bottle and he was fast asleep, I drove back and left him on your doorstep. I watched from a safe distance away and saw you pick him up and take him inside."

"Wouldn't you be able to keep your baby? Couldn't you get better security around this place? It didn't take Ettie and me very much effort to get inside here."

She shook her head. "These people are professionals. If they want to get someone, they'll find a way. And I can't go through it again. We never planned for another baby. He was an accident. I didn't want to go through any more pain after Langley was taken from us."

"We have to tell you that a man came to our house and said he was the father of the baby and asked us to hand him over," Elsa-May said.

The woman gasped and covered her mouth. "I wonder if Craig's found out." She jumped to her feet and took hold of a framed photo that had been sitting on the mantle. "Is this the man?"

Elsa-May shook her head. "No, that's not him. Is that your husband?"

"Yes. That means they know where he is and they're trying to do this all over again."

"I think we might need to get the police

involved," Ettie said. "We got the man's plates and our retired detective friend found out his name and he's got a criminal record."

Tears brimmed again in the woman's eyes. "I feel so helpless. I thought he'd be safe with the Amish."

"You can't continue to live in fear of these people."

"I can't risk my baby's life. I'll do anything, if it means he'll be safe. I can't lose another child."

"While your child is safe, it might be a good time to talk with the police so they can catch these men, and then perhaps when they catch them, you can find out what happened to your first baby."

"Yes, I'd like to know what happened to him and where he is. I want him to have a proper burial. He had a memorial service, but that's not the same. He's lying out there somewhere—all by himself." She shook her head and through tear-filled eyes said, "How did they find him? I was being so careful. Not even my husband knew about the baby."

"Didn't he see you getting bigger and think it strange that you were gone for so long?"

"I told him my sister was sick. My sister knew, of course, but she'd never tell anyone anything. We've always held each other's secrets since we were children." She went on to remind them, "It was my husband's fault that we lost Langley. If he'd just done what the kidnappers said, we'd have gotten him back."

"But you don't know that for certain," Ettie said.

"In my heart, I know it. Things were never the same between Craig and me after that. He'll be so upset with me if he learns about the baby. I suppose I've got to tell the police about it now. If they know my baby exists, and it sounds like they do, he won't be safe."

"Do you want us to call the detective for you? The one who came here was retired, but we do know a real one quite well," Ettie said.

"Would you?" Mrs. Cohen asked.

Ettie stood up. "Where's the phone?"

The woman stood up and pointed to the phone in

the corner of the room.

"I'll phone Detective Crowley," Ettie muttered, being too afraid to talk to Detective Kelly herself. She'd call Crowley and then he could call Kelly and fill him in. While Ettie dialed the number, Elsa-May continued to talk with Genevieve. Knowing Crowley's mobile number by heart, Ettie dialed.

"Hello?" Crowley answered.

"It's Ettie."

"Where are you phoning from, Ettie?"

"I'm at Genevieve Cohen's place and she's agreed to co-operate. She got very worried when she learned that a man had come to our door asking for the baby."

"He's *her* baby?"

"Yes, he is."

"Good work, Ettie, I'll get in touch with Detective Kelly right away."

"Elsa-May and I will leave before he gets here."

"Yes, that might be a good idea. Thanks again, Ettie."

Ettie hung up thinking he'd already finished

talking. *Did he just thank me?* Normally he warned them to keep out of things, but that was before he'd retired.

"All done?" Genevieve asked Ettie as she approached.

"Yes. Detective Kelly should be here soon."

Elsa-May rose to her feet. "We'd better go, then."

"Yes, we should and we need to hurry," Ettie said, fearing the lecture Kelly would give them. He wouldn't be as lenient as Crowley.

"Are you certain my baby is safe?" Mrs. Cohen asked when everyone was standing.

"My grandson is newly married and he's taken the day off to look after Luke with his wife."

"Luke? You've named him?"

"We thought we should give him a name."

"I didn't give him a name because I knew I couldn't keep him. I hope something works out so I can. That would be my best dream come true. Perhaps the police will catch these people."

"We will pray for the best outcome," Ettie said.

"Thank you, both of you."

Ettie leaned in and quietly asked Mrs. Cohen, "Who's the woman who answered the door?"

"She's my personal secretary, Nerida."

"What's her last name?"

"Flower."

"Nerida Flower," Elsa-May said. "How long has she worked for you?"

"I couldn't be without her. She's worked for me for nearly ten years. She kept the household going while I was away."

"Does she know about the baby?" Ettie asked.

"She knows everything about me, but I trust her completely."

After they said goodbye, Ettie and Elsa-May hurried toward the gates. The gates opened as they drew closer.

"We should've called for a taxi before we left the house."

"Too late now. I'm not staying there any longer so Kelly can see us."

"Why are you so scared of him?" Elsa-May asked.

"He always makes me feel guilty of something. And he always says that we're sticking our noses into things."

Elsa-May chuckled. "Come on. Let's walk this direction. There are some stores up here and there should be a public phone where we can call for a taxi."

"What do you think of Nerida?"

"She looks a little cranky."

Ettie shook her head. "I don't know. I think she might not be as trustworthy as Genevieve thinks."

"Why don't we see what we can find out about her?"

"We will."

Chapter 9

Ettie and Elsa-May had been home for two hours before they got a knock on the door.

Ettie looked out the window. "It's Detective Kelly."

"I suppose we should let him in. I hope he's not mad with us for contacting Crowley instead of him."

"Me too." Ettie shrugged off her nervousness and opened the door to Detective Kelly, with Elsa-May standing right behind her.

He looked at both of them. "Good afternoon."

"Good afternoon, Detective," Elsa-May said.

Ettie stepped back. "Come in."

"Ow! That was my foot, Ettie."

Ettie spun around. "Oh, sorry."

Elsa-May shook her head and looked at Detective Kelly. "Can we make you some tea?"

As he moved toward the living room, he said, "I'm in no mood for tea."

Ettie exchanged nervous glances with Elsa-May.

"We did the right thing in telling you about the baby," Ettie said to soften his mood.

He sat carefully on one of their wooden chairs.

As Elsa-May sat in her usual chair, she said, "It's all right. We've had the chairs fixed. They're quite safe now. Not that they weren't safe before...."

"I didn't come here to talk about your furniture." He glared at Elsa-May, and then he turned his head and glared at Ettie.

"As I was saying, we told you about the baby."

"No you didn't. You went to Genevieve Cohen's house without her permission—as good as trespassed, and then you contacted Crowley rather than me. And when did you find the baby on your doorstep? Crowley said it was yesterday."

"That's right," Elsa-May said. "We did what we thought was right for the baby, and what his mother wrote in the note."

He pressed his lips tightly together. "Where is he now?"

"He's with friends of ours and he's safe."

"You know I'm going to have to contact social services, don't you?"

"Can't you hold off doing that? Genevieve Cohen said she didn't want *Englischers* to take the baby. She's happy to leave him with us. She said…"

"This time, I'll do what you ask, but only because Mrs. Cohen also requested that I hold off as long as possible before contacting social services. She'd like nothing more than to take her baby back, as long as it's safe to do so. Since her first baby was taken from her home four years ago, she feels better that this baby is elsewhere."

"That's good that she wants her baby back," Elsa-May said. "She left him here for a good reason."

"I've got Victor Lemonis in for questioning. He's the man who came here asking for the baby. So far, he hasn't talked. I'm going to go back to the station after I talk with the pair of you. I'll do my best to get some information out of him."

"That's good," Ettie said.

"The good news is that the cold case unit is now

following up on the old kidnapping of Langley Cohen and we're working closely with them. And next time anything like this happens you must contact me directly. Crowley is retired. You need to call me and not him."

Ettie nodded, feeling like she was back at school when the teacher would reprimand her for daydreaming. "Yes, Detective Kelly."

"What do we do now?" Elsa-May asked him.

"As far as the baby is concerned, we're looking at things one day at a time. Crowley suggested having your grandson and his wife approved as temporary custodians, and that should be fine since we have Mrs. Cohen's approval."

"So she said the baby can stay with Ava and Jeremiah?"

"We'll have to wait and see. There are charges for abandoning a baby—it's a crime and Mrs. Cohen will have to face those charges."

"I'm sure she only did it for the best reasons," Ettie said.

"All that will be taken into consideration and

she's had previous psychiatric care and will need to be evaluated again. I'm holding off on her arrest because I don't want to draw attention to the case while we're investigating it."

"So she will be charged at some point?" Elsa-May asked.

"Yes she will, but I'm putting it off for as long as possible. Now that we've got Victor Lemonis we're hoping he'll lead us to his accomplices."

"I hope so. Jeremiah is bringing the baby back here tonight."

"And he's going to stay here too because that's the arrangements we've made."

Kelly nodded. "Okay. I'll send a doctor over to check that the baby's in good health. What time will the baby be here?"

"I'd say by six tonight," Ettie said, glancing at Elsa-May who nodded in agreement.

"Leave it with me," the detective said, rising to his feet.

"Can we trust this doctor will be confidential?" Ettie asked.

"The doctor will be on a need-to-know basis. Don't mention anything about the baby. All I will be asking of him is to give the baby a check-up and make sure he's all right. Give him any story you want. Anyway, I doubt he'll ask anything. That baby's health is my primary concern at this point in time—understood?"

Ettie and Elsa-May nodded and walked Detective Kelly to the door.

When Ettie and Elsa-May were by themselves, Ettie looked at Elsa-May and asked, "What do we do now?"

Elsa-May wiggled her shoulders and threw her hands in the air. "I suppose we just wait here until Jeremiah comes back with Luke. And then wait for the doctor."

"I'm not comfortable with a doctor coming here, but what do we do?"

"Neither am I, Ettie, but I suppose it's a compromise."

Chapter 10

Jeremiah knocked on the door and walked in with the laundry basket. Ettie and Elsa-May rushed to him.

"How is he?" Ettie asked as she peered into the basket.

"He's good. He's just been fed and he's gone back to sleep."

"The detective has arranged for a doctor to check him over."

"Crowley?"

"*Nee* Kelly."

"What happened today?"

"Put Luke in the bedroom and then we'll tell you all about it."

When the three of them were sitting in the living room, they told Jeremiah everything."

"So they've got the kidnapper, then?"

"*Jah,* they're trying to get a confession out of him and find out what happened to the Cohens' first baby."

"I hope he tells them."

"*Jah*, it must be awful not knowing the truth of what happened."

"Kelly said we're not to tell the doctor the true circumstances of the baby. He said we could make something up, but…"

"I don't want to do that," Jeremiah said.

"*Nee,* we didn't think that you would. Hopefully, the doctor won't ask a thing. He'll simply be here to give the baby a quick check-up to make sure he's healthy."

"Of course he's healthy; anyone can see that," Jeremiah said.

"I suppose the detective is just playing it safe—playing it by the rules. Mind you, I do think he's bending them a little in these circumstances," Elsa-May said.

"He should, too, considering all that poor Genevieve Cohen has been through," Ettie added.

When a knock sounded at the door, Ettie pulled the curtains aside to look out. "Looks like that's the doctor."

"Can you take him to the baby, Jeremiah?"

"Act like he's yours," Ettie added.

Jeremiah frowned. "I'll not lie."

Ettie raised her eyebrows. "We're not asking you to, are we, Elsa-May?"

Elsa-May shook her head. "Why don't you answer the door, Jeremiah, and stay with the doctor while he looks the baby over?"

"Okay." Jeremiah answered the door and took the doctor through to Ettie's room where the baby was, while Ettie and Elsa-May sat on the couch.

"It was good of Detective Kelly, I suppose, not to charge Mrs. Cohen right away."

"Shh," Elsa-May said.

"I didn't say it loud enough for anyone to hear me."

"All the same, don't talk about it—wait until the doctor leaves."

Ten minutes later, Jeremiah escorted the doctor past the ladies and the doctor merely nodded to them. Jeremiah opened the door for him and thanked him for coming. When Jeremiah closed the door, Ettie and Elsa-May were right next to him.

"Well, what did he say?" Elsa-May asked.

"He's healthy. He just said to continue what we're doing for the cord. It's nearly all dried up now."

Ettie breathed out heavily. "Good. That's a relief."

"What do we have for dinner, Ettie?" Elsa-May asked.

Ettie pulled her mouth to one side. "We do have plenty of leftovers from last night."

"That's fine by me," Jeremiah said. "I liked it last night and I'll like it again tonight."

"Elsa-May?"

"Fine."

"Gut! Now did the doctor ask you any questions, Jeremiah?" Ettie asked.

"Nee, except he asked how the mother was and I said that she was good."

"Excellent. *Gut* work, Jeremiah," Elsa-May said

as she patted him on his arm.

Ettie went back to the window and peeped out again and, just like Kelly said there would be, there was a plainclothes police officer in a car parked right outside the house.

"What is it?" Elsa-May asked.

"I'm guessing that is a policeman sitting in that car."

Elsa-May nodded. "Kelly said he'd have someone in the street watching the house all night."

"I'm sure that'll give Genevieve peace of mind that her baby is being watched so closely. It's sad that she'll be charged for giving him up," Ettie said.

"Well, it's the way she did it, Ettie. She could have found someone to raise the baby and adopt him through the proper channels, but as Kelly said, people just can't drop their *kinner* off somewhere and leave them."

"I know, Elsa-May, I know. No one would be able to understand the grief that she's already been through." Ettie wiped a tear from her eye.

"Don't start. You'll have me crying," Elsa-May

said.

"I'll reheat the meal." Ettie headed to the kitchen. It was a rare thing to see so much emotion from Elsa-May, since she'd always seemed so strong and in control.

Chapter 11

During the night, Ettie woke to an intruder coming through the front door. At first she thought she'd been dreaming the scratching and rattling sounds, but when she realized she was sleeping on the couch and a man was in the house, she screamed as she came to her feet.

Before she drew breath to scream a second time, Jeremiah came running out from the other end of the house, and someone came through the front door and jumped on top of the first man.

"Don't move! Police!" Ettie heard someone shout.

Jeremiah turned on a gas lantern to see someone being placed in handcuffs. When the man on the floor was yanked to his feet, Ettie saw it was the same one who'd come to the door the other day—the suspected kidnapper—Victor Lemonis.

"Ettie, are you all right?" Jeremiah asked.

Ettie plopped back down onto the couch when

her legs gave way from under her.

"Everyone okay in here?" the policeman asked.

"I'm okay," Ettie said. "Are you okay, Jeremiah?"

"Yes, and Luke's safe; I'll check on Elsa-May."

Ettie was worried that Elsa-May hadn't run out when Jeremiah had.

Jeremiah came back just as the policeman was taking the intruder out. Ettie looked out the window to see more than one police car. Lemonis had to be the kidnapper coming back to get the child.

When Jeremiah came back out he said, "Elsa-May is still asleep and she's snoring."

"She slept through the whole thing?"

"It seems like it."

"Lock the door will you, Jeremiah? I hope they'll still keep a policeman outside. We won't know who else might be lurking about."

"Yes I'm sure they will. If not, I'm here." Jeremiah walked closer to Ettie. "Are you sure you're all right?"

"It's just the scare, that's all."

"Would you like me to make you a cup of hot

tea?"

"Jah, I'd love a cup, *denke."*

"Coming right up," he said before he headed to the kitchen.

Ettie propped pillows behind her. Then she lifted her legs out in front of her and covered them in her warm blanket.

Ettie must've closed her eyes because the next thing she knew it was morning, and a shaft of light was shining through the gap in the curtains. She sat up when she noticed Elsa-May in her chair. "Did you hear what happened last night, Elsa-May? Unless I dreamed the whole thing."

"Nee you didn't. Jeremiah told me that Lemonis came into our *haus* and the police took him away. I'm surprised I slept right through the whole thing."

"Where is Jeremiah?"

"In the kitchen giving Luke his bottle."

"We'll have to call the police station and find out if he told them what happened to the poor baby he kidnapped before. I hope he confessed and then maybe the Cohens can finally find some peace."

"Why don't we phone them after breakfast?"

Ettie agreed, but before they even had a chance to start on breakfast, there was a loud knock on the door.

"That's Detective Kelly," Ettie said.

"How do you know that without even looking?"

"I know his knock," Ettie stood up.

"Just be sure first, and check out the window."

Ettie peeped out the window and saw Detective Kelly. Instead of the dark crumpled suit he usually wore, he was wearing a white shirt with gray baggy pants and sneakers. He looked like he hadn't had any sleep. Ettie put her robe on, and then placed her prayer *kapp* on top of her head, tucking in her two long braids.

"Are you going to open the door in your dressing gown?" Elsa-May asked.

"Why not? It's morning and besides, it's warm." She opened the door and Kelly asked if he could come in.

"Of course."

Once he was further inside, Jeremiah came out

of the kitchen with Luke in his arms.

"I think you'll all need to have a seat." Kelly's brow furrowed deeply.

"What's wrong?" Elsa-May asked.

Ettie hoped he'd say that nothing was wrong but he remained stony-faced.

"Can I listen, too?" Jeremiah asked, to which the detective gave a nod. "I'll put the baby in his basket. I won't be a minute."

When Jeremiah returned and they were all seated in the living room, Detective Kelly drew in a deep breath.

Elsa-May leaned forward. "What is it, Detective Kelly, you look dreadful."

"I'm wondering where to start. You obviously found out that we let Victor Lemonis go after hours of questioning. We had nothing to hold him on, so we had no choice but to let him go. We followed him, hoping he'd lead us to someone who might have helped him with the kidnapping all those years ago. At the very least, we hoped that he'd lead us to someone who would be able to help with our inquiries."

"He came here to get the baby again," Ettie said. "This time he wasn't going to ask, he was just going to take the baby."

"We let him go and followed him here. We alerted Jeff, the officer who was stationed outside your house. After we arrested Lemonis for breaking and entering, we took him back and locked him up again. This time we had him on a charge so we could keep him for longer than the maximum twenty-four hours. When we were going to start a new round of questioning, I'm afraid we opened the cell and made a grisly discovery.

"What?" Elsa-May asked.

Kelly's shoulders slumped. "He'd done away with himself."

"He's dead?" Ettie asked, not believing her ears.

Kelly nodded. "I'm afraid so."

Ettie pulled her dressing gown high around her neck. What Kelly had told them didn't seem real.

"Last night, we prematurely told the Cohens that we were onto something and that we were certain we'd apprehended one of the kidnappers. Then we had to tell them this morning what had happened. They were devastated. They had hopes that they'd finally find out what happened to their baby all those years ago. Now there is a real possibility that we'll never know."

"How did it happen? I thought prisoners were searched for things they might harm themselves with before you put them in the cell," Elsa-May asked.

"He hanged himself with his shirt."

Ettie covered her face with her hands. It was too awful to think about.

"These things happen all too frequently. Often it's not the hardened criminals who kill themselves. I remember one time it was a solicitor who was caught skimming funds from one of his company accounts. It was the shame of having to face charges and go to jail. Another time it was a company executive on speeding charges. He was held in the cell for three hours and he killed himself."

"That's horrible," Jeremiah said.

"It's something that's in the forefront of our minds and that's why we have suicide-proof cells, but I guess if someone's going to do it, they'll find a way. It's hard to tell if someone's going to try to do it or not. Often we can't tell."

"Why would they take their own lives?" Ettie asked. "People make mistakes and learn from them."

"According to psychiatrists, they think they've ruined their lives. Then they're concerned about what their family and friends will say." He shook his head. "We haven't had a suicide in years. It's hard to deal with when it happens. We're supposed to look after them while they're in our custody. They're our responsibility—we failed him."

Ettie stared at Detective Kelly as he hung his head. "Would you like something to eat? We can fix you some eggs, and we've got coffee ready."

He lifted his head and smiled. "I'll start with a cup of coffee, thanks. The police department runs on coffee."

Chapter 12

They all moved to the kitchen and Ettie fixed Kelly some eggs while he drank his coffee.

"What happens now with the investigation? Does it end there?" Elsa-May asked.

"We're getting a warrant to search his car and his house. We'll take any cell phones and computers and go right through them. We're sure to find some evidence. Do you know what people in jail do to kidnappers and people who hurt children?" Kelly asked Elsa-May.

Elsa-May shook her head.

He shook his head. "I can't tell you, I'll leave it to your imagination. Often they have to go into protective custody, but just the thought of what Lemonis would face was enough to make him kill himself."

"What happens now with the baby?" Jeremiah asked. "I have to work today. He'll be with my wife, though, if you want me to take him again."

"I would prefer he stay here today. I'll have two men sitting in a patrol car all day."

"Is the baby still in danger?" Ettie asked handing Kelly a plate of scrambled eggs and toast.

"We can't be certain about anything until we find out exactly what happened with Lemonis. We need to find his accomplices."

"What if he didn't have any?"

"He would've had someone in on it with him—at least one and maybe two others. It's too big a thing for someone to pull off on their own."

When Jeremiah left, Ettie sat down at the table with Kelly and Elsa-May.

"Have you had any sleep?" Ettie asked Kelly.

"I've had a couple of hours. That'll be enough. I might grab a couple more during the day. I prefer to see this through. When the warrant comes through, which should be just after nine, we're going to go directly to his house and take his car."

"Are the cold case people still working with you?"

"They are, and they bring with them some

excellent detectives." Kelly spooned a large forkful of scrambled egg into his mouth. "Although, I remain the head detective on the case."

"That's good. I hope some peace will come to the Cohens soon."

"So do I," Kelly said. "Thank you for breakfast. This will keep me going and I'm hoping we get some major breakthroughs today."

Some time after Kelly had left, Jeremiah delivered Ava back to the door.

"Ava, have you come to help us with Luke?"

"I certainly have. I know it can be tiring looking after a young baby and I thought you might appreciate some help." Ava giggled. "And I was so disappointed when Jeremiah told me that I wouldn't be looking after him today."

When Ava came further into the house, Ettie closed the front door behind her. "Did Jeremiah tell you everything that happened last night?"

"*Jah,* he did. It was terrible what that man did to himself. And it must've given you such a fright when he came into the house like that."

Ettie heard a car drive up and stop outside her house. She looked out to see a police car and another car stopped behind it. "What's going on now?"

"What is it, Ettie?" Ava asked.

"Police! And a woman is getting out of the car behind them."

Elsa-May nudged Ettie out of the way. "It looks like a social worker."

"Come to take Luke?" Ettie's jaw fell open. "Kelly said he'd give us time."

"I'd say our time has run out," Elsa-May said, staring out the window.

"Stop it!" Ava said to Snowy who was pawing at her leg.

Ettie answered the door. "Are you looking for me?"

"We're here to take the baby. Are you Ettie Smith?"

"I am."

"Detective Kelly didn't have time to come here and tell you himself and he said to apologize for that. This is Mrs. Watkins, a social worker. She'll take the baby with her."

Elsa-May leaned forward. "Detective Kelly said he wasn't going to call the social worker just yet. He promised to give us a little bit of time looking after him."

"Mrs. Cohen has requested her baby be returned to her and Mr. Cohen."

Ettie gasped and looked at Elsa-May. Why couldn't she have come there and taken him back herself?

Elsa-May pushed herself up off the couch and stood next to Ettie. "Does she get him back just like that? She left him alone and it could've rained on him. What if she leaves him somewhere again?"

The social worker said, "When something like this happens, our aim is to have the mother take the baby back. Then we monitor them closely, and she'll have ongoing counseling."

"Will she still be charged?" Elsa-May asked the officer.

He nodded. "There are charges pending. Now,

the baby?" The officer looked at each of the three ladies in turn.

"I'll fetch him," Ava said, walking toward the bedroom.

"I do hope Mrs. Cohen makes a full recovery. It can't be easy for her after what happened. I'm sure what she did was with the very best intentions," Ettie said, hoping her words would calm Elsa-May.

"Don't be concerned. We'll be watching her closely," the social worker assured her.

Ettie nodded. "That's good."

Ava came to the door with the baby and told the social worker Luke's routine.

"Shouldn't you be writing this down?" Elsa-May asked the social worker.

The social worker raised her thin eyebrows. "Oh yes. I'll just get my notebook out of the car. If you don't mind waiting."

"We'll wait right here," Ava said.

"Before we hand the baby over, can we see some form of identification?" Ettie asked the officer.

The officer whipped his badge out of his pocket

and showed them.

"You don't mind if we make a phone call to Detective Kelly to verify you being here?" Elsa-May asked.

"Not at all," he said.

Ettie took the mobile phone that Crowley had loaned them for emergencies and then looked through her address book. When she found Kelly's personal mobile number, she dialed it.

"Crowley, what can I do for you?" Detective Kelly answered.

"It's not Crowley. It's Ettie Smith. Crowley loaned us his phone in case of emergencies."

"Is there anything wrong?"

"There might be, if you didn't send an officer and a social worker to our house."

"I did, Mrs. Smith, and I didn't have time to let you know in person, and I apologize for that. I should've, under the circumstances but it's been hard to get away from the station. Mr. and Mrs. Cohen want their baby back, and we had to get the social workers involved. I know you've got concerns and so do we, that's why they'll be carefully monitoring mother and baby."

"Okay, thank you, Detective Kelly. We're handing the baby over right now."

"Very good, Mrs. Smith. I do thank you for your help and I will keep you informed of any updates."

"Thank you." Ettie pressed the 'end call' button, and then turned the phone off and placed it back in the drawer of the bureau where they had been keeping it.

When the social worker and the police officer drove away with Luke, Ava burst into tears. "I'm sorry for sniveling like this. It's just that I grew attached to him."

"Why don't we go into the kitchen," Ettie said. "I'll make you a nice cup of hot tea."

Denke, Ettie. I thought I'd be able to have all day with him and now he's gone."

"I understand. We'll all miss him."

"While you two drink tea, I'll take Snowy for a walk."

"You do that, Elsa-May," Ettie said with her arm around a sobbing Ava as she guided her to the kitchen.

Chapter 13

Twenty minutes later, when Elsa-May walked back through the door with Snowy, she had two large pumpkins in her arms.

Ettie looked up from her seated position in the kitchen. "Pumpkins!"

"Where did they come from?" Ava asked.

"From the man next door. He often gives us fruit or vegetables when he has too many."

"I guess it's pumpkin pie and pumpkin soup for dinner?" Elsa-May asked.

"That sounds nice," Ettie said. "Why don't you and Jeremiah stay here for dinner, Ava?"

"You don't mind?"

"Of course, not. We'd love you to join us."

"Well that will save me cooking, and I asked Jeremiah to pick me up when he finishes work, which would be about six or six thirty."

"Sounds perfect. I'll have dinner ready and waiting," Ettie said.

"I don't think I've ever made pumpkin pie," Ava said.

"You can help me then and that way you'll learn."

Ettie tried her best to take Ava's mind off the baby and what kind of life he'd have. She'd certainly grown attached to Luke in a short space of time.

When Jeremiah came to collect Ava that evening, they had dinner and then dessert.

Just as Ava and Jeremiah were about to leave, Crowley came to the door.

"Come in," Elsa-May said to Crowley.

After he'd greeted everyone, he sat down in one of their wooden chairs next to Jeremiah and Ava, who were already seated. "Ah, you've had them fixed." He hit the side of the chair.

"Yes, didn't we tell you that?" Elsa-May replied. "Jeremiah fixed them."

Crowley managed a smile in Jeremiah's direction.

"What's wrong?" Ettie asked from the couch.

He looked up at Elsa-May who was still standing. "Sit down, Elsa-May, I've got an update."

"You don't look too happy," Ettie said.

"Is Luke all right?" Ava asked.

Crowley nodded. "The baby's fine. Kelly told me the baby was returned to his mother and father. Anyway, I stopped in at the station to see what they'd found out so far. When the kidnapping was being investigated years ago, I was at the station, but it wasn't my case, and then it was taken over by the FBI."

"Yes, we know all that. What do you know that's new?" Elsa-May asked.

"That's the problem. So far they've turned up nothing. Kelly's got a team on it, going through Lemonis' phone and his computer. They haven't found a single solitary thing to link him to the kidnapping of the Cohen baby."

"Would he have another phone like you do?" Ettie asked.

"If he did have one, he's thrown it away or hidden it. They've contacted all the service providers—

phone companies—and there are no other phones in his name. At this stage of the game, it looks like all his secrets might have died with him. It's a real blow to the case. Now we could very well have nothing, unless one of the evidence technicians finds something from his apartment, but so far there's nothing."

"That would be a real disappointment to Genevieve Cohen."

"Yes. Anyway, Kelly asked me to stop by and keep you informed. He'll have patrol cars going by your house for the next few nights just to keep an eye on the place."

"I'm sure that's not necessary. Shouldn't they be patrolling the Cohen household?"

"Mrs. Cohen and the house are being watched closely in case there is another kidnap attempt."

"So you do think the man came here with the intention to take the baby?" Elsa-May asked.

"He asked you for the baby. And that's the only reason we have for assuming he had something to do with the Cohen kidnapping."

Elsa-May stared into space.

"What are you thinking, Elsa-May?" Ettie asked.

"What if he didn't have anything to do with it?"

"Then why did he kill himself?" Ettie asked her sister. "And why did he come here asking for the baby pretending to be his father?"

"Kelly told us that many people don't need a good reason to do away with themselves. What if he thought the kidnapping was going to be pinned on him and no one would believe his innocence. Detective Crowley, you said once that there are many innocent people in jail—that the system often gets things wrong."

Crowley raised his eyebrows. "Elsa-May could be right. Someone could've paid him money to say he was the father and collect the baby and that was as far as it went. To prove his innocence, he might have had to point the finger at the guilty people. He might have feared them even more than he feared death."

"It's a possibility, but where does that leave things? And, if he wasn't guilty of the first kidnapping, what possible reason would he have to turn up on our doorstep demanding the baby?" Ettie asked.

"Didn't you hear what Crowley just said? He said that someone could've paid him to get the baby and say he was the father. Like the man they found taking the money in the first kidnapping, he might not have known anything," Elsa-May said.

Ettie nodded. "I see."

"It's a very different thing—collecting money and taking a baby," Crowley said. "But I think it has to be considered."

"Hasn't it been a short amount of time to go through his phone and his computer? I thought that would take days and days."

"There is a team of people working on it. If there's a good lead they should've come across it quicker than that. The man had only been out of jail for eight weeks. So they would've only had eight weeks' worth of telephone data and emails to go through."

"What was the length of the term he was

imprisoned for?" Ava asked.

"Three years."

"So was he out of jail at the time of the kidnapping of their first child?" Ava inquired.

"He was, yes."

"Would you like a slice of pumpkin pie?" Elsa-May asked Crowley.

His face lighted up. "I'd love some. I've missed your cooking."

"Ettie made it."

He chuckled. "Your cooking is good too, Ettie. More than good."

Jeremiah stood up. "We should go, Ava." He touched Ava on her arm and she stood, too.

"I might stop over tomorrow and see how things are going," Ava said.

After they both left and Elsa-May was cutting the pie, Ettie leaned over toward Crowley. "Was there anything you couldn't tell us in front of them?"

He shook his head. "No. It's a huge disappointment and a frustration that we can no longer ask Lemonis questions. I mean 'they,' since

I'm now retired. Even though I'm retired, cases like this still pull me in. I'm sure the Cohens will want to find where their baby is so they can lay him to rest properly."

"You think he's dead?"

"It's unlikely they'll find him alive. That's what happens, unfortunately, when kidnappers don't get their money."

Ettie shook her head. "Who could kill an innocent baby?"

"These people aren't wired the same as you and me."

"Who's not?" Elsa-May came out of the kitchen with a plate of pie and handed it to Crowley.

"Thank you, Elsa-May. Ettie was just asking about the baby who was kidnapped four years ago. I said he would be dead and she found it hard to believe someone could harm an innocent child, but I'm afraid awful things do happen."

Elsa-May sat heavily in her chair. "That's worse than awful. I don't like to think about it."

"The Cohens had to come to terms with it, but

knowing that his remains are out there somewhere would be a strange feeling. They'll feel a sense of peace if we can at least find out what happened to him. Finding his remains would be the best outcome."

"It's not looking likely that you'll find out, though, is it? There are no other leads?"

"What about the people Lemonis was in prison with?"

"That's being looked into, but there are many people that he would've come in contact with, so it's a slow process."

"I do hope they'll find some kind of clue amongst his things," Ettie said biting the end of a fingernail.

Crowley had a mouthful of pumpkin pie so could only nod in agreement. "It's certainly a mystery," he said once he'd swallowed.

* * *

Once Crowley left, Ettie said goodnight to Elsa-May and went to her bedroom. In her room, she saw that the baby basket was still on top of her dresser. It was the same baby basket that his mother had left him in on their doorstep.

Ettie untied her prayer *kapp* and tossed it on her nightstand, hoping that young Luke would be okay. Had his mother simply made an error in judgment? What she did was not the actions of a sane woman. And what did Mr. Cohen think of suddenly finding out he was a father for a second time? He must've adjusted well to demand the baby back unexpectedly like that.

Ettie unwound the braids that kept her hair in place under her *kapp* and then she brushed out her gray hair. Once she changed into her nightgown, she slipped between the covers. Had anyone asked any questions of Mr. Cohen? What if he were somehow involved? Was it an elaborate plot to hide money from the IRS? *No money was taken, though. But maybe he'd planned that it was to have been and he hadn't meant for his baby to be harmed.*

"*Nee,* if he'd had any involvement he would've

seen that his baby was returned."

Elsa-May stuck her head through Ettie's door. "Did you say something?"

"I was just thinking out loud."

"You can't 'think' out loud, Ettie, that's called talking."

Ettie giggled. "I was thinking and then talking—to myself."

"Are you all right?"

"Nee."

"That's what I thought," Elsa-May said.

"I'm just worried about Luke."

"We can pray for Luke and his family."

"Jah, I'll be doing that. And praying that they'll find out what happened to their first baby."

Elsa-May shuddered and leaned against the door. "It's so awful thinking about things like that."

"It must be dreadful for the Cohens, not knowing what became of Langley. It's been four years already. Now the only person the police have found that might know something about him has gone."

"Not 'might know,' Ettie, he would know

something about it. If he wasn't directly involved, he would know who told him to come here to get the baby."

"I suppose that's right."

Elsa-May sighed heavily. "We'll just have to wait and hope that they find some evidence soon."

Ettie pulled her covers up higher.

"I'm off to bed as soon as I clean those last dishes."

"Sorry, I completely forgot about them."

"I'll do them; I'm not ready to go to sleep yet," Elsa-May said.

"Good night."

Elsa-May turned away and waved a hand in the air as she left the room.

Ettie didn't like to admit it, but she couldn't help feeling scared about intruders coming into her home after the fright Lemonis had given her. Part of her wondered if Elsa-May felt the same and that's why she was staying up later than normal. To give voice to her fears would've made her feel a whole lot worse, so she pulled the covers over her head and prayed in the darkness.

Chapter 14

Early the next morning when Ettie and Elsa-May were having breakfast, there was a knock on their door.

"I hope that's Kelly telling us they found something," Ettie said. "You stay here; I'll go and see."

"Be careful," Elsa-May said.

"I will," Ettie sang out just as she reached the window. It was Ava and Jeremiah.

Ettie opened the door. "Hello, you two."

"I'm sorry to visit again so soon, but Ava wanted to stop by and see if the police have found anything out."

Elsa-May came out of the kitchen. "Good to see you both again. Have you eaten?"

Jeremiah walked forward, "We have."

"Come and talk to us in the kitchen."

They all sat around the kitchen table.

"All we can do now is wait to see what they find

out," Ettie said before she slurped her tea.

"Ettie, you're slurping again."

"Well, you do it too."

"Not since you told me to stop because it irritates you."

"All right. I'll stop then since you've been good enough to stop."

Elsa-May nodded. *"Gut!"*

"I didn't take time off from work to hear about slurping," Jeremiah said.

Elsa-May raised her eyebrows and fastened her eyes on Jeremiah. "You're still my grandson, Jeremiah, even if you are fully grown. If I want to talk about slurping, I will."

"Sorry, Elsa-May," he said with a hint of a smirk on his face. He looked at Ava. "I've been told."

Ava giggled and then said to Ettie, "You never wait—I mean—you've never waited around before when you found dead people."

Ettie pushed her lips out. "I don't know what I can do."

"Investigate like you did on the murders."

"She's right, Ettie. We've never waited around before; we've always been more active. Except that time I was in the hospital and you had to find out things yourself. Then there were the times I had to stay home with Snowy. But all those times you found things out by yourself."

"Ettie can't do anything dangerous like that," Jeremiah said.

"We'll help, won't we, Elsa-May?" Ava said.

"Of course we will. Now let's figure this out with the information we have so far."

Jeremiah folded his arms. "Can I make myself a cup of tea while you all talk?"

"Go ahead," Elsa-May said pointing to the pot. "We've just boiled the water. You'll need to put it on the stove again but it won't take long."

Since everyone seemed confident in her, Ettie took the lead. "Here's what we know so far. The Cohens' baby was kidnapped four years ago. No one knows who did it and the only lead they have was the man who said he was paid to pick up the money. They caught him at the drop-off zone with the money, and then when they questioned him, he knew nothing and the Cohens never got their baby back."

Elsa-May took over, "Then Mrs. Cohen found she was expecting again, against her husband's wishes. Without telling him about the pregnancy, she went to her sister's place in Canada to have the baby. When she came back, she left him at our door. That very day, a man came asking for the baby, saying he was the father, and then we found out he was Victor Lemonis."

Ettie took over again, "He was found, questioned and when he was released, he tried to break into our house—presumably to steal the baby."

"He broke in—he didn't *try* to break in," Elsa-May corrected her.

"What would you know? You slept through the whole thing," Ettie said.

"Snoring too," Jeremiah added with a teasing smile as he sat back down at the kitchen table.

Elsa-May frowned at Jeremiah, and he looked away from her and took a sip of tea.

"Those details aren't important. Anyway, after he broke in here, he was arrested and taken back to the station where he was placed in a cell, and then he killed himself. Have I left anything out?" Elsa-May looked around at everyone. They all shook their heads.

Ettie breathed out heavily. "It looks like Lemonis is not guilty of the kidnapping, and it looks like he had no reason to come here and ask for the baby, so why did he?"

"He must've met with someone in person who instructed him to come here to steal the baby," Jeremiah suggested.

"Possibly he was innocent like the first man the kidnappers paid to collect the money for them," Ava said.

"That is an option," Ettie said. "Anyone else got any ideas?" Everyone remained silent. "We'll have to look at what Jeremiah said. Who would've been likely to have Lemonis come and take the baby?"

"The same people who took the first baby?" Ava asked.

"Could be likely," Ettie said. "What if we try to find people who've committed other kidnapping crimes?"

"That would be a point to start with," Elsa-May said.

"How could we do that? We don't have all the crime information that the police can tap into," Jeremiah said.

"I thought you were staying out of this, Jeremiah." Elsa-May stared at her grandson.

"I am. I'm just offering a suggestion. Well, not really a suggestion, more of a comment."

Ava said, "We do have court case information on the Internet. When I was at college, I did a law course and we had a site where we could access court records. Now that I'm not a student, though, the only access I'll have is information arranged by date, so it would take forever to go through them all."

Jeremiah frowned at Ava. "You went to college?"

Ava's lips turned down at the corners. *"Jah,* I'm sure I told you that."

"Nee, I don't think you did." He shook his head.

"You two can argue about that later. What about newspaper articles?" Elsa-May suggested.

"I like it," Ettie said.

"Most of those should be on the Internet," Ava said.

"I can drive everyone to the library," Jeremiah said.

"There's no need," Ettie said. "Crowley left us a cell phone for emergencies and it's one of those iPhones where we can get onto the Internet."

"Quick, go and get it, Ettie."

When Ettie brought the phone into the kitchen, Jeremiah sprang to his feet. "I hope you're not going to turn that thing on under your roof, *Mammi?"* He glared at Elsa-May, his grandmother, and then glared at his great-aunt.

Ettie and Elsa-May looked at each other.

"Perhaps we should go to the library?" Ava suggested. "If you take us to the library, Jeremiah, then you can go back to work."

"Okay," Elsa-May said, "We'll go to the library."

Ettie said, "You're such a stickler for rules, Jeremiah. It'll save time if we look it up here and now! The bishop won't mind if it's saving someone's life. I'll confess to the wrongdoing myself if that eases your conscience."

Jeremiah folded his arms tightly in front of his chest. "If we ease up on one rule we might as well ease up on the lot, and where would that leave us? We must follow the *Ordnung* and the guidance of the bishop."

"I suppose you're right," Elsa-May said.

"It's probably best we go to the library and it's not that far," Ava said.

"Come on, Ettie, let's just go there," Elsa-May said.

"Very well," Ettie grumbled.

Chapter 15

Jeremiah stopped the buggy not far from the library. "It's a bit of a walk, but I can't stop any closer."

"This is fine, Jeremiah, *denke,*" Elsa-May said before she stepped down.

"I'll see you all later."

When Jeremiah drove away, Ettie said to Ava, "I hope we haven't gotten you into trouble."

Ava winced. "He doesn't like to do anything that might be considered questionable. With him, it's all black and white and nothing in between. I thought I told him I went to college, but it sounds like I didn't. He'll think my education has made me prideful."

"Well you aren't, so don't concern yourself. I guess that's the way he feels safest—to be cautious and that's not a bad way to be," Elsa-May said as they headed toward the library.

"We'll let you do the looking up on the computer,

Ava, since you know what you're doing better than either of us."

"Okay."

When they found a free computer, Ava pulled two extra chairs beside her. Ettie and Elsa-May sat close at either side so they could see the screen.

"Search for kidnapping in this area and see what comes up," Elsa-May ordered.

After a few minutes of searching, Ava said, "There are a few women who have stolen babies, but no one taking babies for money yet."

"Keep looking," Elsa-May said. "Unless one of those women is… What was that woman's name, Ettie?"

"Mrs. Cohen personal secretary?"

"Jah, I don't trust that woman—she looked shifty."

"I think her name was… it was something odd. I wish I'd written it down. Was it Jemimah or something?"

Elsa-May frowned. "Nerida Flower—that's what it was."

"*Gut* work, Elsa-May. I should've remembered a name like that."

"I'll look up her name when I finish this search," Ava said. "Write it down so you don't forget the name."

Ettie obeyed and wrote the name down.

Ava peered at the screen. "There are plenty of news articles on the Cohen kidnapping four years ago. but they aren't telling me anythng we don't already know."

"Skip them and move on," Ettie said.

"Okay. There's a movie about a woman who was abducted as a child and how she adjusts when she comes home."

Ettie huffed. "Focus, Ava, focus."

Ava frowned. "Okay, but it looks interesting."

"You're not going to watch it so move on. You don't want to give Jeremiah something else to grumble about," Elsa-May said.

"You're right." Ava giggled. After looking for a few more minutes, Ava said, "There doesn't seem to be anything here."

"Increase the search into other areas," Elsa-May suggested. "Go wider."

"All right. The whole of Pennsylvania?"

"Jah, the whole of Pennsylvania," Ettie said.

"Here's something." Ava straightened her back. "Oh no. It's another movie. Sorry."

"That's okay, keep looking," Elsa-May said rubbing her head.

"I wonder how many children are kidnapped and we never hear about it. Mrs. Cohen's husband was the one who got the police involved; if it had been solely up to Genevieve, she would've paid them the money and kept silent," Ettie said.

"So you're saying that maybe these kidnappers have never been caught and they might have done it before and even after?" Elsa-May said.

Ettie nodded. "It's a possibility."

"Should we be looking at unsolved cases, then?" Ava asked. "Or people suspected of something, but never charged?"

Elsa-May said, *"Jah,* if we can find people like that. Let's have a look at them before we go further."

Ava pulled up a list of unsolved cases and after Ettie and Elsa-May had read a couple of them, they didn't want to read more. All the children that had been taken were either found dead or were never found at all. In one of the cases, a man had given a deathbed confession that he'd kidnapped a child, but he gave no more details as to what had happened to that child.

"This is too gruesome," Ava said.

Ettie said, "Ava, I want you to write down every name that a newspaper has mentioned of being connected to a kidnapping. Then find a photo of them and print them all off."

Ava nodded. "Okay, it might take some time. I'll have to print each one separately and write their name on the same page."

"We've got all day," Ettie said.

"What are you going to do with their photos, Ettie?" Elsa-May asked.

"We're going to visit Mrs. Cohen again and show her the photos to see if she knows one of them."

"Why would she?"

"I don't know, but this is all we've got so far. You all wanted me to do something, so I'm doing something."

Elsa-May leaned forward and jutted out her bottom jaw. "I meant something that would lead to a result."

"A little silence please, so I can concentrate," Ava said in a small voice.

Ettie frowned at Elsa-May, shaking her head.

When Ava was through, there were twenty photos of men, who were at some point, alleged kidnappers. Ettie carefully studied each photo before she passed them to Elsa-May.

"See anyone you know?" Ava asked.

"Nee, no one looks familiar to me," Ettie said.

"Now we'll have to get a taxi to Mrs. Cohen's house."

Are you coming with us, Ava?"

"I wouldn't miss seeing Luke; of course I'll come."

"Wait!" Ettie said. "See what you can find out about Nerida Flower."

"Okay." Ava turned back to the computer and searched the woman's name. "There's nothing here. Nothing that I can find out about her, and she doesn't even have Facebook."

Elsa-May said, "Facebook's for younger people, isn't it? She seems to be around fifty."

"That's young to me," Ettie said. "So nothing at all?"

"Nothing. But..." Ava continued, "wait a minute. Hand me those photos."

Elsa-May handed the photos of the possible kidnappers to Ava.

Ava pulled one of the photos out. "I thought that name was familiar. Look here! Kel Flower."

"Ah! I wonder if they are relatives," Elsa-May said.

"I wonder if the police have missed that. They would've checked everyone out—everyone who was close to the Cohens, that is," Ettie said.

"This will make the visit to Mrs. Cohen even

more interesting," Elsa-May said.

"Could you phone a taxi for us, Ava?" Ettie asked.

"Jah, what's the address?"

When Elsa-May gave her the address, Ava headed off to the front of the building where the pay phones were.

"I hope Mrs. Cohen talks with us," Ettie said to Elsa-May.

"She should. She talked to us the other day."

"I suppose so."

"She'll want to find the kidnappers. So she can feel safe."

Chapter 16

The taxi dropped the three ladies off at Mrs. Cohen's house, and Elsa-May led the way to the tall front gates and then she pressed the intercom button.

"What is she doing?" whispered Ava.

"That's where you talk to someone inside when you arrive in a car."

Ava and Ettie watched as Elsa-May talked to an employee within the house. "We're here to see Mrs. Cohen and she'll want to see us. It's a matter of vital importance. Just tell her three Amish ladies are here to see her."

A minute later, the gates opened and the three ladies hurried through them. Their feet crunched along the tiny white pebbles that led toward the front steps of the house. Before they reached the door, it opened and Mrs. Cohen stood there staring at them.

"I'm so pleased you've come. Do come inside,"

she said once they drew closer.

Ettie introduced Ava and told Mrs. Cohen that Ava had taken good care of her baby for one of the days that they'd had him. Once they were sitting down, Mrs. Cohen told them that the baby was asleep upstairs and was nearly due to wake.

"I would so like to see him now that I'm here. I miss him so much," Ava said.

Mrs. Cohen smiled kindly at her. "Of course, I'll take you up in a minute. Have the police made any inroads yet?"

"Their only suspect, Victor Lemonis, killed himself, and without him, I don't know if they've got anything to go on. Detective Kelly tells me he's hopeful of uncovering evidence from his apartment," Ettie said.

"I've heard all about it from the detective," Mrs. Cohen said with a frown.

"Mrs. Cohen, it's only a slight chance, but do any of these men look familiar?" Elsa-May handed the stack of photos to her.

"Take your time," Ettie said.

She looked at the photos one by one and hesitated at one man, and then looked up holding the photo high. "This man did my gardening for a while."

"Are you certain?" Ettie asked, hoping it would be the man whose last name was Flower.

"Yes. I could track down his name. Or do you know it?" Mrs. Cohen asked.

"Ava? Do we know his name?" Ettie asked.

"It's written on the front in small pencil writing." Ava stood up and studied the photo. "George Cousins."

"That's him. I remember he worked here for around six months, but I had to get rid of him."

"Why's that?" Ettie asked.

"He pruned my roses way too much."

Ava asked, "Did your baby go missing from the house here? We never heard how or where he went missing from."

She nodded. "He was taken at night from this very house."

"He would've known the routine of your household—I'm guessing," Elsa-May added.

"I suppose he would've, but at the time the police asked questions of everyone who'd ever worked here. They questioned my current and past staff—I'm certain of it. Where did you get the photo of him?"

"From the Internet. He's been suspected of kidnapping before," Ava said.

Mrs. Cohen drew her fingers to her throat and gasped.

"Ettie, you should call Detective Kelly," Elsa-May said.

"Can I use your phone?"

"Yes, it's over by the window."

Ettie called Detective Kelly and told him what they'd found out. She hoped this lead would prove to be of value otherwise Kelly would be furious with them for butting in and wasting his time.

"He's coming here right away," Ettie said once she'd hung up. "There is one more picture that I'd like you to take a good look at, Genevieve."

"Okay."

Ettie found the photo of Kel Flower and handed

it to her.

Genevieve Cohen looked at it hard, and then shook her head. "I don't believe I've ever seen this man before. Who is he?"

"Just... don't worry. He's no one."

"Just another man who might have possibly been involved in a kidnapping," Elsa-May said.

Mrs. Cohen handed the photo back.

"Where is your secretary today?" Ettie asked.

"She's sick today, and then she has tomorrow off. Which works out well because I don't want her anywhere near the baby when she's sick."

"She's not *too* ill, I hope," Elsa-May asked.

"She's got a cold, and she couldn't stop sneezing this morning, so I told her to take the day off. She's not left her apartment all day."

Ettie nodded. "She lives nearby?"

Mrs. Cohen raised her eyebrows. "She lives in the servants' wing." Mrs. Cohen laughed. "I know it sounds pretentious—we don't call our employees servants, but that's what they called that section of the house when we purchased the property ten years ago. It's more of a self-contained apartment adjoining the house, but that's quite a mouthful to say."

"Could I have a quick look at the baby?" Ava asked.

"Yes, he's upstairs. I'll take you now." Mrs. Cohen led the way, and they all followed her up the stairs. When she reached the landing, she turned around. "My husband is getting used to the idea of another baby, but we don't have a proper nursery yet. We're keeping him in the upstairs study until the decorators come and turn it into a nursery." She pushed a door open. "There he is. I don't think he's awake."

The three of them peered into the crib to see Luke sleeping soundly.

"He looks happy to be home," Elsa-May said quietly, turning to Mrs. Cohen.

"I hope so. And I hope he'll forgive me when he grows up and finds out what I did. I don't think my husband will forgive me. He's coming around; he never wanted another baby after what happened before, and neither did I."

"You did what you thought was best," Ettie said.

"That's not what the police think. I'm going to be charged for leaving him."

"Are you?" Elsa-May asked, acting shocked, as though she hadn't heard that before.

Mrs. Cohen nodded.

"I'm sure they'll take into account your extraordinary circumstances. And the fact that you stayed and waited until I took the baby into the house."

"I hope you're right. It's just another worry. My husband insisted we have a fulltime nanny to help look after Luke. He doesn't trust me anymore—I'm sure that's why he wants a nanny here."

"You're leaving his name as Luke?" Ava asked.

Mrs. Cohen smiled. "I think it suits him well, but we're leaving off the traditional 'k' and the 'e,' and spelling it with a 'c.' That's what we put on his birth certificate, 'Luc." It's the French spelling, I believe, and I have a penchant for all things French."

French or not, Ettie hid her dislike of the name Genevieve had chosen for the baby. Surely that name would be mixed up with the female name of Lucy. She didn't like that idea at all, but she kept silent, as it wasn't her choice to make.

Chapter 17

A loud buzzing sounded.

"That's the intercom," Mrs. Cohen said. She called out to someone they hadn't seen before, "Jill, if that's the police, let them through."

Ettie's heart beat wildly, hoping that she was helping rather than hindering the investigation. If she were hindering it, she'd never hear the end of it.

"Who's Jill?" Ava asked.

"She's my housekeeper. We don't have a nanny yet; we're still interviewing." Mrs. Cohen moved into the hallway and looked out a window at the driveway below. "It's the police. We should head downstairs. Watch Luc would you, Jill?"

A small dark-haired woman appeared out of an adjacent room. "Yes, Mrs. Cohen."

The three women walked down the stairs behind Mrs. Cohen who then opened the door to Detective Kelly, who had another plainclothes man standing beside him.

Ettie, who was standing a distance back from the door, could see them in the doorway. She whispered to Elsa-May, "I'd say that's the man who's heading up the cold case unit."

"Could be," Elsa-May whispered back.

When Kelly walked through the door, he introduced the other man as Detective McDonald from the Cold Case unit.

"We'll sit down in the sitting room. Come through this way," Mrs. Cohen said.

Ettie had thought they'd already been in the sitting room, and was amazed at how many rooms there were in the house. The sitting room overlooked the rolling green grounds of the hedge-walled back yard. There was a pool to the left and what appeared to be a pool house next to it.

"Thank you for your call, Mrs. Smith," Kelly said to Ettie in a low voice.

After they had all sunken into the soft white leather couches, Kelly leaned forward and said to Ettie, "Can I take a look at the pictures you showed

Mrs. Cohen?"

"Ava," Ettie said.

Ava handed over all the photos they'd printed off at the library.

After he leafed through them with Detective McDonald looking on, he handed them to Genevieve Cohen. "Which man do you think was working for you?"

She picked her way through them until she found the one. "Here." She handed it to the detective. "This man definitely worked here as a gardener."

"And this is his name?" Kelly pointed to the penciled name.

"His name is George Cousins. He was never a good worker. I gave him chance after chance, but he just wouldn't follow instructions. I had no choice but to let him go after he butchered my roses. I grew them from seeds that I'd brought all the way back from France. I can't replace them. They've recovered now, but it's taken years."

Kelly said to McDonald, "Have you come across him before?"

"He was in the file as someone who was questioned, but he had an alibi. We'll take a closer look at him and his alibi."

"Good. Thank you, Mrs. Smith and… everyone."

Ettie felt a weight off her shoulders. She wasn't in trouble like she thought she might be.

McDonald jumped to his feet. "Excuse me, I need to call someone to get onto things right away." He strode out of the room and made a call from the hallway.

When McDonald came back into the room, Kelly said he'd be in touch with all of them and then both detectives left.

"Well, we shouldn't hold you up any longer," Ettie said to Mrs. Cohen.

"I'm not doing anything important. Ava, shall we go up and see if Luc's awake yet?"

"Yes, I'd love to have another hold of him if I could."

"We might wait here, if that's okay," Elsa-May said. "We're too old to go running up and down stairs. Once a day is enough."

Mrs. Cohen smiled. "Why don't you go through to the kitchen and I'll have Jill bring you a cup of hot tea if you're not in a hurry?"

"Sounds good to me," Elsa-May said.

"The kitchen is down the hall and to the right."

Ettie nodded hoping that tea would be accompanied by cake or at least cookies—she was starving and it was a little past their regular time for the midday meal. "I would like to see Luc again, but I do feel a little faint."

"As soon as we leave here we'll get something to eat somewhere."

It was a rare occasion that Ettie and Elsa-May were thinking along the same lines.

When they heard a car, Ettie looked out the window. "The gates opened by themselves so this might be Mr. Cohen." When the car drove into a four-car garage next to the house, they knew it was Mr. Cohen.

"Has he come home for lunch I wonder?" Elsa-May said.

"He might work at home some of the time; many

people do."

They watched the man leave the garage and walk through the doors of the kitchen. He was a small portly bald man—nothing like Ettie had envisioned Mrs. Cohen being married to.

"Hello?" he said as he closed the sliding door behind him.

"Hello, are you Mr. Cohen?"

"I am," he said looking slightly amused.

Ettie introduced herself and Elsa-May to him and let him know how they knew Mrs. Cohen.

"Your wife is upstairs showing the baby to one of our friends."

"You're the ladies Genevieve left our baby with?"

"We are."

"I don't know how I can thank you for taking such good care of him."

"It was our pleasure to look after him." Elsa-May smiled.

"We did the best we could," Ettie said.

"My wife has been under tremendous pressure—

we both have. I've got my company to keep me busy, but my wife has no distractions and she constantly dwells on the past."

"It would be something difficult to forget. I can't imagine going through something like that," Ettie said.

He nodded.

Jill appeared. "Tea, Mr. Cohen?"

"Will you join me, ladies?"

"Yes we will, thank you."

He handed his briefcase to Jill. "Put this away for me first would you?"

"Yes, Mr. Cohen." Jill disappeared with his briefcase while Mr. Cohen sat down at the table with Ettie and Elsa-May.

"There's been a development that you might not know about," Ettie said.

"Well, it might be a long shot—or a tiny piece of a large puzzle. I'd hardly call it a development yet, Ettie."

He stared at them. "What is it?"

"One of your gardeners from years ago was

implicated in another kidnapping."

"The police questioned him at the time, but he had an alibi," Elsa-May added.

"They questioned him about my first son going missing?"

"Yes, when they were questioning everyone. Detective Kelly said that they questioned all your past and current employees." Ettie nibbled on her thumbnail wondered if Kelly had said that or if she'd heard it from someone else.

He sprang to his feet. "I'm going to call Kelly right now and get the facts. He said he'd keep me up to date with everything."

"It's only just happened," Ettie said, hoping he'd change his mind about calling Detective Kelly.

Mr. Cohen ignored Ettie's comment and pulled his phone out of his pocket and paced up and down while talking to Kelly.

Elsa-May leaned over to her sister, and whispered, "Nice work, Ettie. If Kelly wasn't mad at us before he will be now."

Ettie shrank down further in her seat while Jill

came back into the kitchen and filled up the electric kettle.

When Mr. Cohen hung up the phone, Ava and Mrs. Cohen appeared with the baby in Mrs. Cohen's arms.

"There he is," Mr. Cohen said as he took hold of the baby.

In her heart, Ettie knew that Mr. Cohen couldn't have had anything to do with the disappearance of his first baby four years ago, and she was ashamed of herself for recently thinking otherwise.

Mrs. Cohen introduced Ava to her husband and then asked Jill to heat Luc's bottle. Ettie felt a little sorry for Jill who appeared to have to do everything around the place.

While Mr. Cohen fed the baby his bottle, they sat around the kitchen table eating smoked salmon sandwiches on soft white bread with the crusts cut off, and small round tasty cheese cookies.

"Do you mind if I hold the baby before we go?" Ava asked before she gave an embarrassed giggle. "I love babies and can't wait to have one of my own."

Before Mr. or Mrs. Cohen could answer her question, Mr. Cohen's cell phone sounded and without saying anything, he handed the baby with his bottle to Ava before he stood.

Ettie guessed it was Kelly on the phone by the concerned look on his face. "Very good. Be sure to call me back and let me know what happens." He ended the call and sat down. "That was the detective. He said that man who used to do the gardening for us was in the same jail at the same time as Victor Lemonis was in jail. He said he's going to pick him up and then they'll question him and take things from there." He turned to his wife. "He said depending on how things go, you might have to make a positive ID on him."

"Me? No. I don't want to do that. I've already told him that's the man who worked for us."

Mr. Cohen shrugged. "I guess we have to do whatever they say."

Mrs. Cohen's face grew dark and angry like a storm cloud ready to release a lightening strike.

"Look what happened last time you trusted the police."

Mr. Cohen remained silent, but his face went beet red.

Ettie said, "Well, we should be going now. We've taken up enough of your time."

Elsa-May pushed herself to her feet. "At least now they'll be sure to check on his alibi again."

"Bye, little man," Ava said softly to the baby before she handed Luc back to Mrs. Cohen.

"Thank you once again ladies—all of you. We owe you a great deal. If there's anything we can ever do for you, please let us know," Mr. Cohen said rising to his feet. "I'll walk you out."

* * *

"Well *that* was awkward," Elsa-May said once they were outside the gates.

"At least we got fed," Ettie said.

"And again, we forgot to ask for them to call a taxi. We'll have to walk up to the shops again."

"It's not that far," Ettie said.

"The man didn't seem very nice to his wife," Ava said.

"I thought he was okay," Ettie said.

"They've both been under a lot of pressure since the baby was kidnapped. And what his wife did, hiding the fact that they'd had another baby, would've been like Mr. Cohen losing another baby all over again. Imagine if he hadn't found out for ten years and he would've lost all those years. Even though he said he didn't want another one, he obviously didn't mean it—look at him now. He adores that baby."

"Seems so, Elsa-May," Ettie agreed.

"What do we do now?" Ava asked.

"All we can do is go home and wait," Elsa-May said. "Wait, and pray that Detective Kelly and Detective McDonald uncover the truth."

"I do hope they keep a better watch on the man when they put him in the cell. We don't want to lose another man who knows something about the kidnapping," Ava said.

"I'm sure they will, Ava," Elsa-May said.

"And there is something else we could do," Ava said.

"What's that?" Ettie asked.

"We could find out more about Nerida Flower."

"And how would we do that?" Elsa-May asked.

"We follow her and see where she goes."

"How? We don't have a car."

"I could see if my friend, Lydia, will drive us. She's between jobs at the moment. We could offer to pay her for her time and that would be cheaper than a taxi."

"I guess we could do that, but do you think we should've told Kelly that her last name is the same as a suspected kidnapper's?" Elsa-May asked.

"That's it, Elsa-May! We tell Kelly that tomorrow morning, early. Then Kelly will question her immediately because he gets onto things quickly. And then if that man—Kel—is a relative of hers, she might go to see him to tip him off that they're onto him."

"I like it," Elsa-May said.

Ettie turned to Ava. "Do you remember your friend's phone number?"

"I'll call directory services and get her home number. She lives with her parents and I'm certain she'll be home."

"Sounds like a plan," Elsa-May said, "but you mustn't tell your friend what it's all about."

Ava nodded. "I won't."

Chapter 18

Ettie and Elsa-May waited near the public phone while Ava made the call to her friend to see if she would be able to drive them around the following day.

The sisters overheard Ava's side of the conversation.

"It sounds like her friend is agreeing."

"It certainly does sound that way," Ettie agreed with her sister. "Ava was right; a taxi would've cost us a fortune."

"There is every possibility that Nerida Flower won't leave the house all day especially since she's been sick."

"Well, if she is a relation to Kel Flower there is every possibility that she'll try to contact him."

"That's what we're hoping."

Ava hung up the phone. "She said she'd do it, and she's going to pick us up from your place at eight o'clock in the morning. She said that's very early for her because, since she's been out of a job, she hasn't been waking up till eleven or twelve."

"Humph, that's the waste of a day," Elsa-May said.

Ettie agreed, "Half the day would be gone."

"She's agreed to do it and I said we'd pay her gasoline costs."

"That's only fair," Ettie said.

"We'll pay her for her time too," Elsa-May said.

Nee, Elsa-May, there's really no need. She's not doing anything else and she's happy to do it."

"Okay." Elsa-May nodded.

"Are you going to tell Jeremiah what we're doing tomorrow?" Ettie asked.

"Not unless he asks me, which he probably won't. I'll have him bring me over early in the morning before he starts work."

"Good idea," Ettie said.

"Now we should call for a taxi to get home." Elsa-May stepped toward the pay phone.

* * *

The sisters had the taxi driver take Ava to her place before they were delivered home. When Ettie and Elsa-May walked through their front door, Snowy came bounding towards them.

Elsa-May leaned down and lifted Snowy up, but he was wriggling too much, so she had to put him down again. "I'll guess I'll have to take him for a walk to use up some of his energy."

Ettie stood looking around the house with her hands on her hips. "And while you're doing that, I'll clean up. Look at this place; it's a mess! I haven't seen it like this since I don't know when."

"We've had a lot going on, we've had the baby, then Jeremiah staying here, and Ava coming 'round. Crowley and Kelly have been coming here at all different times, too, so we haven't had time to think—let alone clean the house."

"I know, but I feel irritated when the house is messy. I'm going to clean it up right now."

"I'll help when I get back," Elsa-May said as she clipped the leash onto Snowy's collar. "I'm going to cook chicken and roasted vegetables for dinner and, while that's cooking, I'll help you clean up."

"Gut! That's my favorite." Ettie walked into her bedroom and pulled the sheets off the bed.

Now there were loads of sheets to wash. There were the sheets she'd pulled off the bed so Jeremiah could have fresh sheets—the ones she'd been using—and then there were Jeremiah's sheets that he'd used. That was two pairs of sheets, top and bottom sheets, and four pillowcases since Jeremiah and she liked to sleep with two pillows each.

With the intermittent rain, she wondered when the sheets would ever dry. Back when she lived on her farm, her husband had made her a wet-weather line by the barn—she'd hang the washing under cover when it was raining and the wind would dry it.

With the small house she now shared with her older sister, there was nowhere to dry the clothes in the wet weather. Sometimes they'd used a portable clothes rack and dried things in front of the fire, but it looked so unsightly.

Ettie threw the sheets inside the gas-powered

washing machine and closed the lid. She'd get to it tomorrow. Out of the linen cupboard, she pulled another pair of fresh sheets and made up her bed.

"That looks much better," she said standing back and looking at the made bed. Her eyes went to the floor. The next thing she had to do was run a broom over the entire house. With this rain and people coming in and out of the house, there was no point washing the floor just yet, but it certainly needed a good going over with the broom.

Just when she was sweeping up the collected dirt with a dustpan and brush, Elsa-May arrived home.

"Finished cleaning yet?" she asked as she bent down and set Snowy free. Snowy ran directly to Ettie sending the dustpan and all the dirt flying.

"Elsa-May!" Ettie yelled. "Your dog!"

Elsa-May leaned down, picked him up and put him outside. "No need to be like that. You were the one who wanted me to get the dog."

"I didn't know he'd be so annoying."

"I told you; dogs are a lot of hard work. You just have to learn to have more patience like me."

Elsa-May's comment made Ettie laugh. Ettie swept up the scattered dirt. "At least lock the dog door?"

"Certainly." Elsa-May leaned down and clipped the lock on the door. "Now I'll put the dinner on and then I'll help you. We'll get this place spic and span in no time."

"Denke. That would be good; it would make me feel so much better." Once Ettie tipped the dirt into the trashcan, she moistened a rag and dusted everything in the living room. When that was done, she moved on to their small bathroom and started scrubbing.

It was fifteen minutes later that that Elsa-May came out of the kitchen. "All's under control in the kitchen for the moment. Where would you like me to start, Ettie?"

"The windows. I think you can start cleaning the inside of the windows. They haven't been done for a while. I noticed the front ones are dirty."

Ettie passed Elsa-May one of the rags that she had poured methylated spirits on, and then passed her the bottle. "Here use this; this is the best." A few minutes later, Ettie was lost in her own world thinking about her old days on the farm when Elsa-May called to her.

"Ettie!"

"What?"

"It's Crowley; he's getting out of his car now."

"I'm coming," Ettie yelled back. She threw the rags into the bathtub and washed her hands.

Elsa-May was standing at the door waiting for him, and Ettie came and stood behind her.

"Hello, ladies," he said smiling.

"Do you have good news for us?" Elsa-May asked.

"Come inside," Ettie said worried the neighbors would overhear something. It was bad enough that the neighbors had probably seen police cars there the last couple of days and nights. None of them had said anything, but Ettie knew they would have noticed and been wondering what was going on.

When Crowley was seated, Elsa-May said, "Have you heard the latest from Kelly?"

Crowley nodded. "I was just over there. There's been a break in the case. They found George Cousins and it's thanks to both of you."

"Has he confessed?" Elsa-May asked.

Crowley shook his head. "Not yet, but it's only a matter of time before he does."

"Do you have any evidence on him? I know he was in jail at the same time as Lemonis and that he used to be Mrs. Cohen's gardener, but that doesn't make him guilty." Ettie stared at Crowley.

"It's all of that combined, Ettie. It's a huge coincidence. If it looks like a duck and it quacks like a duck, it's usually a duck."

"We're looking for a kidnapper, not a duck. Do you mean if he doesn't confess he can't be arrested?" Elsa-May asked.

He sighed. "You two are hard work. I'm sure Kelly's got something up his sleeve. You ladies don't need to concern yourselves."

"If Lemonis wasn't involved maybe Cousins isn't involved either. Who does that leave, if that is the case?" Ettie asked.

Elsa-May said, "Did you ever check into Mrs. Cohen's credit card records?

"I did, and you know what I found?" Elsa-May shook her head.

He formed his thumb and forefinger into an 'O.' "A big nothing. What made you think there would be something in her credit card details?"

"I asked you that," Ettie said.

"There was something that seemed a little strange, but nothing to do with the kidnapping case."

Elsa-May leaned forward. "What was it?"

"There were thousands of dollars spent at a furniture store. I followed up with the store and found it had all been delivered to an address in Canada, which may have been her sister's address. I haven't looked into things any further."

"So she gave her sister a gift of furniture?" Ettie asked.

Crowley rubbed his chin. "Was it a gift or was it blackmail for the sister keeping silent about the baby and not telling Craig Cohen?"

"If that were the case, I would feel very sorry for Mrs. Cohen. She wouldn't have felt safe anywhere," Elsa-May said.

"She spoke of her sister as though they were very close, remember, Elsa-May? She said something along the lines of they had 'both kept each other's secrets.'"

Elsa-May scoffed. "Whatever that means."

Crowley shook his head. "She might have simply spent $30,000 on her sister as a gift to show her appreciation."

"$30,000?" Ettie gasped.

"The Cohens are very rich, Ettie. $30,000 to them would probably be like $300 to us."

"$300 is a lot to us," Elsa-May said.

Crowley stared at Elsa-May. "Cup of tea?"

"Of course. Why don't we all go and sit in the kitchen? It'll be a lot warmer in there with the oven on."

They all moved to the kitchen and as Ettie filled up the pot with water, she said to Crowley, "I suppose you're not having much chance to play golf in this weather?"

"We still play when it's raining. I don't personally like to, but my golf friends still play in the rain." He chuckled.

"You've got a girlfriend?" Elsa-May asked, looking surprised.

Crowley looked shocked and then Ettie said to Elsa-May, "He said golf friends, not girlfriend." Ettie frowned at her older sister.

"I don't know why you look so shocked about the idea that I might have a girlfriend, Elsa-May. I'm not dead yet."

She leaned toward him. "You don't have to answer this if you don't want to, but I've always wondered what happened between you and Ettie's daughter, Myra?"

"Elsa-May! That's none of our business." Ettie had just put the pot on to boil and then she sat down at the table with them, glaring at Elsa-May.

"That's all right. I don't mind answering your question. I expected one of you to ask me about her sooner or later. The thing is, everything seemed to be going fine and then all of a sudden she disappeared. I hadn't heard from her in months, and she wasn't taking my calls. When she finally answered her phone, she told me she'd been overseas on a retreat."

"On a retreat? What kind of a retreat?" Elsa-May asked with her chin held high noticeably not liking the sound of whatever it was.

"A meditation one, from what I could gather. She was talking about meditating and talking to some guru—it was a new-age thing." He looked at Ettie. "You haven't heard from her?"

Ettie shook her head. "The only time I hear from Myra is when she's in trouble. When I don't hear from her, I know she's all right. Wherever she is, whatever she's doing, I just have to trust God that she is okay."

"It must be hard," he said. "I've never had any children of my own, as you know. That's one thing I regret in my life. Anyway, I must admit that Myra was one woman who turned my head and that hasn't happened to me since."

"Have you told her so?" Elsa-May asked.

"I would've thought she knew how I felt."

Ettie glared at her sister not believing she was being so intrusive into Crowley's life. Sure, they'd known him for a long time, but they'd never delved into his personal life like this.

Crowley shrugged his shoulders. "The last thing she said to me was that she couldn't speak to me about our relationship until her chakras were aligned."

Thinking Myra's problem was the distance they lived apart, Ettie was certain that a chakra must have been a car-part. "She had a fairly new car, but I suppose things can still go wrong. Surely you could've given her the name of a good mechanic?"

Crowley laughed. "Ettie, chakras haven't anything to do with cars. It's to do with some points on our bodies that you can't see and these points are called chakras."

"So, she's not well?" Elsa-May asked.

Crowley grimaced. "She's well physically, but she thinks she's messed up spiritually—no offence to you Ettie since you're her mother. These chakra points, I think, are some kind of spiritual points. That's the best I could find out anyway. I tried to find out about them and I'm still left uncertain." He shook his head.

"So she's on some kind of spiritual quest. Is that what you're saying?"

"Exactly, Ettie. And when she finishes what she's doing and whatever journey she's on, I just have to think if it's meant to be she'll come back to me, and if she doesn't, it wasn't to be."

"Well, it's none of our business, but I hope things work out for you both," Ettie said.

"That's the water boiling, Ettie," Elsa-May said.

When Ettie got up to make the hot tea, she heard Elsa-May ask Crowley to stay for dinner.

"Are you certain?" he asked. "I don't want to put you out."

"Yes, we're certain. We've got more than enough.

Chapter 19

After dinner, Ettie and Elsa-May whispered together about whether they should tell Crowley what they had planned for the next day. Crowley sat in the living room, and the sisters were discussing their options in the kitchen.

When Ettie and Elsa-May came out with a tray of tea, Crowley said, "Are you two up to something?"

Ettie licked her lips and looked at Elsa-May. "Well, we were discussing if we should tell you something."

"And the way you let our secret out last time makes us think that maybe we shouldn't."

"Nonsense! Whatever it is, I'll be able to help you. You'd never have been able to keep that baby a secret, and look at him now. He's at home with his mother and father where he was meant to be. I'd say that was a pretty good outcome."

Elsa-May shook her head. "But we still don't know for certain who did the original kidnapping."

"We've got leads. All's not lost," Crowley said.

Ettie and Elsa-May stared at each other, and then Elsa-May looked back at Crowley and said, "Okay. This is what we're planning on doing…"

Crowley sat forward in his chair. "Go on."

"We found out that Mrs. Cohen's personal secretary who has worked for her for years has the same last name as someone who was implicated in a kidnapping case."

"How did you find this out?"

"We found him on the Internet the same as we found George Cousins. Mrs. Cohen didn't recognize his photo, of course, but what do you think about her secretary having the same name as a suspected kidnapper?"

"Is she married?"

"We don't think so." Ettie looked at Elsa-May who shook her head.

"We thought we'd tell Kelly early tomorrow morning, and then we figure he'll go and question the secretary, and then we'd follow her to see where she goes."

"You're assuming a lot of things. You're assuming that this person who has the same last name is guilty. Also, that they are related, and that the secretary will withhold information. Exactly how are you going to follow her? In a buggy?"

Ettie giggled. *"Nee.* One of Ava's friends said she'd drive us around for the day."

He shook his head. "No one else should be involved. Cancel Ava's friend and I'll drive you."

"Nee! Would you?"

"That seems to be the only way to control you two. If you can't beat 'em, join 'em."

Ettie looked at Elsa-May. "We could call Ava now and have her call her friend. Ava and Jeremiah do have a phone in their barn."

"Okay, I'll go and call her now, and you fill him in on anything that we've left out."

Elsa-May wrapped her black shawl around her shoulders and hurried out the door. Snowy ran inside through the dog door and scratched on the front door, whining.

"She'll be back soon, Snowy."

Snowy ran and jumped on his dog bed in the corner of the room, looking none too happy.

"What else do you need to tell me?" Crowley asked.

"I can't think of anything else. What will Kelly think of us following someone?"

"He won't mind if he doesn't find out. If he does, then that means we're on to something."

"I didn't think of that. That's true."

"What is the woman's name—the secretary?"

"Nerida Flower, and the man we found is Kel Flower."

"It's not an uncommon name—Flower."

"I've never heard it before."

"I have. And does Kel Flower live around these parts?"

"I'm fairly certain he does. The kidnapping he was implicated in was close by here. Are you able to get a tap on Nerida's phone?"

Crowley's jaw dropped open. "Absolutely not! For something like that, we'd need evidence that she's involved. Right now what you've got is virtually nothing. If your hunch pays off, it'd be like me getting a hole in one next time I play golf."

"And what exactly does that mean?"

He shook his head. "Let's just say it's highly unlikely."

"I just feel that we have to do something and that Nerida woman—there's something about her that's just not right. Anyway, drink your tea before it gets cold."

Crowley sipped his hot tea.

Snowy rushed to the door just before Elsa-May opened it and then he pawed at her.

"Get back," Elsa-May said.

"He was worried that you went without him."

"I thought he would've been asleep in his kennel outside."

"Dogs have a sixth sense as far as their owners' movements are concerned, I'm certain of it," Crowley said.

"Is that your chakra telling you that?" Elsa-May asked, as she replaced her shawl on the peg by the door.

"I'll just keep quiet and drink my tea," Crowley said with a laugh.

Elsa-May sat back down. "Ava said she would cancel her friend and she'd be here early in the morning."

"Ava's coming too?" Crowley asked.

"She was in on it from the beginning," Ettie said. "We can't tell her not to come now."

"Okay, I'm just the driver keeping you all out of trouble."

"You did say you'd help us," Elsa-May pointed out.

"I *am* helping you. I've called in several favors for you already."

"Thank you; that's true. It'll be good to see how a professional follows someone," Ettie said to Elsa-May.

"You don't expect to do this again, do you?" Crowley asked.

"Nee!" Elsa-May shook her head. "We just want a quiet life. We didn't ask Mrs. Cohen to put her baby at our door."

He placed his teacup down on the table in front of him. "You both have a way of finding trouble."

Ettie's eyes opened wide. "We don't find it, it finds us."

Chapter 20

Just as Elsa-May and Ettie had planned, Ettie phoned Detective Kelly on his cell phone early the next morning and told him what she had found out about a possible link between Nerida Flower and Kel Flower. Detective Kelly had told her that he'd definitely look into things.

Ava arrived at Elsa-May and Ettie's house at seven thirty and Crowley arrived not long after. Elsa-May had packed a bag of goodies, food and drink, in case they were following someone and couldn't leave the car.

"This is quite exciting," Elsa-May said to Ettie as they walked to the car.

"Don't get too excited, we could be in the car all day waiting outside Mrs. Cohen's house," Ettie said.

"I hope Nerida's not sick in bed. She might be too sick to leave the house," Elsa-May said.

"There is only one way to find out." Ava got into

the back seat of the car.

Elsa-May slipped into the front seat of Crowley's car, while Ettie climbed in the back with Ava.

When everyone had clipped their seat belts on, Crowley turned around and looked at them all. "I just want to say before we get there, that you ladies are going to stand out like a sore thumb. If we have to follow someone, you might have to be ready to duck down when I say so."

"We can do that," Ava said, and then looked at Elsa-May and Ettie. "Will you two be able to do that?"

"Yes, of course, we can," Elsa-May said.

"Off we go, then." Crowley started the engine.

They arrived at the Cohens' house just before eight in the morning. Crowley had parked up the road where they had a clear view of who was coming and going, but not close enough so they would be seen.

"What do we do now?" Elsa-May asked.

Crowley frowned. "We talked about this; it's a waiting game. I thought you understood that we could be waiting here all day."

"Yes I realize that, but it's quite boring just sitting here watching the house. This kind of work is tiresome, just waiting around."

Crowley sighed. "I'll wait until nine o'clock and if nothing has happened by then, I'll give Kelly a call and see where he's up to with things. If he doesn't think it's worth speaking with Nerida at all, then we're wasting our time."

"That's a good idea," Elsa-May said. "That way, we'll know if he's going to talk with Nerida this morning."

"Maybe we should've done that first?" Ava suggested.

"Down! All of you!" Crowley slid down in the seat the best he could. "That's Kelly's car. I hope he doesn't know my car."

"That's good; things are happening," Ava said. "We're a fair distance away, so he shouldn't notice us."

"I hope not." Crowley sat up a little. "I can see him talking into the intercom. Now the gates are opening, and now he's driving through. At least we know now that Nerida isn't going to the station to talk to Kelly. He's come to her," Crowley said.

Ettie raised her head enough so she could peep out the window. "It'll be interesting to see where she goes after this."

"If she does go somewhere at all, that is," Ava said.

"Can we get up now?" Elsa-May asked.

"Oh, yes, sorry about that. But you'll have to get down again when he drives out."

Elsa-May slid back up to a comfortable seated position. "That's good, then."

"We'll have to wait and see," Crowley said.

Kelly was in the house for half an hour before he drove out.

"Here he comes! Everyone get down again," Crowley ordered.

Once Detective Kelly drove away, they only had to wait fifteen minutes before they saw a car drive through the gates. Once again, Crowley ordered the Amish women to duck down before he picked up a newspaper that he'd had pushed between the seats, to look as though he was reading.

"Has the car gone?" Ettie asked after a minute.

"Yes, you can get up now." He started the engine. "I'm guessing that was Nerida, that is, if she's a middle-aged woman with deathly pale skin and dark hair pulled back tightly."

"That'll be her," Ettie said.

"She's in that light blue car just turning the corner now," he said.

"Don't lose her," Elsa-May blurted out.

"I can't get too close, or she'll know she's being followed. I'll have to keep a fair distance back. There will be a chance that I'll risk losing her by doing so, but this is the best way. If I do lose her, I don't want any grumbling or complaining. If I was still on the force, we'd have three cars tailing her, and we'd be able to communicate with each other. This is the best I can do."

"We trust you," Ava said.

"Do whatever you have to do," Ettie said, while Elsa-May was silent.

They followed Nerida for fifteen minutes before Crowley noticed her pick up a cell phone. She drove another fifteen minutes before she stopped at a diner. When she parked the car, she got out, looked around, and then hurried inside.

"What do we do now?" Ettie asked.

"Is she just going there for breakfast or is she meeting someone?" Ava asked.

"She wouldn't go so far away to have breakfast here. It looks like a fairly ordinary diner. She must be meeting someone. And if our guess is right, she's meeting Kel Flower."

"I guess I should call Kelly to see where he's up to with things." He stared at each lady in turn. "Now, you'll all have to be quiet. I'll put him on speaker."

They nodded in agreement.

Detective Kelly answered Crowley's call. "Crowley, how are you doing?"

"Not bad, not bad."

"I hope those old Amish ladies aren't giving you too much grief." Kelly laughed.

Elsa-May opened her mouth in horror and both Ava and Ettie leaned forward and covered her mouth so she wouldn't speak.

Crowley shook his head at Elsa-May and held up his hand in an effort to communicate to her to keep silent. "They're okay. I'm just calling to see where you're up to with things in this kidnapping cold case."

Kelly rattled off the latest, and then he'd checked to see if there was any connection between the suspected kidnapper and criminal, Kel Flower, and Nerida Flower who work for the Cohens. Kelly went on to say, "Turns out, Nerida has a cousin called Kel Flower, but she says she hasn't seen him in years and doesn't know his whereabouts."

"That's interesting," Crowley said. "If I can be any help with anything let me know. I'm not doing much these days."

"Thanks. I'll keep it in mind."

"Okay." Crowley ended the call.

"Did you hear what Kelly said about us Ettie?"

"I certainly did, but that's not what I'm concerned

about right now, Elsa-May. Just ignore it. What he said wasn't too bad."

"Look! That looks like the man from the photo. He's getting out of that yellow car." Ava pointed at the man.

"That's him all right," Elsa-May said. "She said she'd lost touch with him."

"What do you think about that, Crowley?" Ettie asked.

Crowley pulled out his phone. "I think I should take some photos of them talking with each other. You all stay here while I go in and buy something. While I'm waiting, I'll pretend to be reading messages while I take photos of the two of them. And I'm afraid I might have to let Kelly know."

"Know what?" Ettie asked.

"Can't you say that we showed you the photos of the man and then you just happen to be here having breakfast?" Elsa-May asked.

"Let me just get in and get those photos first. I'll figure something out." When he was halfway out of the car, he wagged his finger at all of them.

"You ladies stay here and if anyone comes out of the diner, you put your heads down, okay?"

"Yes," Ettie said.

"Understood," Ava said.

Around twenty minutes later, Crowley got back into the car with a take-out coffee. "I got the photos," he said.

"Did you hear what they said?" asked Elsa-May.

"Were you close enough to listen to what they were talking about?" Ettie asked at the same time.

"No. They did have concerned looks on their faces. It seemed she was telling him the police were asking questions. Of course, that doesn't make him guilty of anything."

"But it does mean that she lied to the police," Ava added.

"She wouldn't be the first person who's lied to the police."

"Quick, get down!" Elsa-May said. "They're coming out."

From Ettie's crouched position in the back seat, she said, "Shall we follow this Kel character?"

"That's a good idea, Ettie. We might as well see where he goes."

They followed Kel's car for half an hour before he turned into a housing estate.

"I'm going to have to turn a different way from him now. If I keep on his tail, he's going to know we're following him." Once they had turned into the estate, the yellow car went left and Crowley turned right.

"I just hope these streets are on a grid system." Crowley drove around, turning down several streets. "No. I think we've lost him. I didn't realize these streets would've had so many dead ends."

"Keep trying," Elsa-May said. "He can't have gone too far. He's in this estate somewhere."

"It looks as though there's only one way in and one way out. I could pull over and look at the GPS."

The next street he turned down, Elsa-May said, "Look! There's the yellow car!"

He drove past to see that Kel Flower had just gotten out of his car and was standing in front of a woman. Then, a little boy ran out to Kel. Crowley had no choice but to keep driving past.

"Did you see that?" Elsa-May asked.

"Yes, it was a boy," Ava said.

"Do you think it could be Langley?" Ettie asked as shivers traveled up and down her spine.

Crowley said, "I wonder. What's the name of the street?"

Ava replied, "I noticed this is Walnut Street, and the number on the house was twelve."

"I'm going to have to tell Kelly. If that's Langley, they'll be on the move now—there's nothing surer."

Crowley pulled his car over, and then forwarded Kelly the pictures of Kel and Nerida before he called him. He managed to leave the ladies out of the conversation and Kelly did not ask how Crowley had come by the information, neither did he ask how Crowley just happen to be at that same diner.

"I'll get someone out there right now," Kelly said before Crowley hung up the phone.

Crowley released a deep breath. He looked at Elsa-May and then glanced back at Ava and Ettie. "I would say that was a day's work well done."

"And it's not even afternoon," Ettie said.

"I can't believe I let you ladies talk me into this." Crowley chuckled and rubbed his face with his hands.

Elsa-May jutted out her bottom jaw. "If I remember correctly, you offered."

"Maybe I did." He grabbed the steering wheel. "I'll take you ladies home, and then I'll drop by the station to see what I can find out."

Chapter 21

Elsa-May was on her way out of the house with Snowy when she saw Genevieve getting out of a car. She stuck her head back inside and yelled to Ettie. "It's Genevieve, Ettie, come quickly."

Ettie hurried out of the kitchen with her heart pumping fast, anxious to hear news of Langley. Was it purely a coincidence that Kel Flower had driven straight to the house of a woman with a small boy who seemed the same age as Langley would've been?

Genevieve Cohen approached after she took her small baby out of his car seat.

"Come in; it's lovely to see you," Elsa-May said with a firm hold on Snowy's leash.

"I hope I'm not intruding, am I? I believe you don't have a phone; otherwise, I would've called first."

"People drop in on us anytime. Everyone does. Come inside out of the cold," Ettie said.

Once Genevieve was seated, Elsa-May said, "I'll put the dog out and wash my hands so I can have a hold of Luc."

"Can I please hold him?" Ettie asked.

"Yes, of course," Mrs. Cohen said.

Ettie took Luc out of her arms. "He's still so tiny and adorable."

"He certainly is. I can't stop staring at him."

"It's a nice surprise that you've come to see us."

When Elsa-May came out of the bathroom, Ettie handed the baby to her.

"I just wanted to come here and thank you ladies for everything you've done. And, I've got a bit of good news—possible good news—that I might be able to tell you."

"What is it?" Ettie asked as she sat down on the couch next to Genevieve.

"The police think they might have found Langley."

"Really?" Ettie asked, acting as though she'd never heard anything about it.

"How did that come about?" Elsa-May asked as

she rocked the baby to and fro.

"I think it had something to do with Nerida, my personal secretary. She up and quit unexpectedly. Then I found out that she's being charged with a number of things. One of them is withholding information and… something like obstructing the course of justice?" She shook her head. "I'm not certain of the exact words, but she had knowledge of the kidnapping. Craig is simply furious."

"That's dreadful! And you trusted her so much," Ettie said.

"What did she know about the kidnapping exactly?" Elsa-May asked.

"From what I know, she wasn't directly involved. She must've known those who were. I feel dreadful that I trusted that woman with my most precious possession—my child. It just goes to show that you can't trust anybody."

"Tell us more about this boy that could be Langley," Ettie said. "What have the police found out so far?"

"He was found at the home of the sister-in-law of

one of the suspected kidnappers. There is no birth certificate for that little boy, and no record of the woman who claims to be his mother ever having given birth to a child. She couldn't produce any paperwork whatsoever. We should know tomorrow or the next day if he's Langley. He's in foster care at the moment. If he's not my boy, he'll be somebody else's, but I'm hoping he's Langley. We're crossing our fingers that he's Langley."

"I'm surprised the police told you all this before they knew for certain," Elsa-May said.

So was Ettie, but she'd kept silent about that, knowing the police must be certain that the boy was one and the same to have told the parents anything about him.

"I don't think they were going to at first, but Craig went down to the station and demanded to know what was going on once Nerida quit and we found out about the police charges against her."

"We'll be praying for you and your husband," Ettie said. "When will you know for certain?"

"In a day or so," Genevieve repeated.

Elsa-May, who'd been busily cooing at Luc, looked up and asked, "What's happening in a day or so?"

"The DNA results will be back. We're not getting our hopes up just yet. We've had too many disappointments."

"That would be wonderful," Elsa-May said, staring at Luc again. "Look at his little face, Ettie."

Ettie stood up and looked down at Luc. "He has to be the cutest baby I've ever seen. He's just so lovable."

"He is, isn't he?" Genevieve said.

"Ava will be so disappointed that she's missed out on seeing him. She cried when he left us that time when the social worker came," Elsa-May said.

"Why don't you have her come 'round, I'm not in a hurry; unless you are?"

"We've nowhere to be. Would you mind waiting?" Ettie asked.

"I don't mind at all."

"She doesn't live that far away. I guess it will take her fifteen or twenty minutes to get here."

"That's fine," Genevieve said.

"I'll call her," Ettie said.

"While you're out, I'll put the pot on to boil. By the time we have cake and a cup of tea, Ava should be here."

"That's if I can catch her at home," Ettie said.

"Fingers crossed," Genevieve said as Ettie headed out the door.

Genevieve talking about fingers crossed was something to do with superstition, which reminded Ettie of what Crowley had said about her daughter, Myra.

Myra had strayed from the path that she was raised on. She was raised to believe in the Bible and to follow the *Ordnung*. But what was to become of her now that she wasn't following the ways of the Lord? Myra was just as lost as Langley, even though she was a middle-aged woman. Yet Ettie knew nothing she could do would change anything—it was out of her hands. Things had been easier when her children were younger—when they listened to what she said and she could protect them. Now that they were older, they no longer needed her and even though she had great grandchildren now, she still found it hard to let go if she thought they were heading in the wrong direction or making bad decisions.

Ettie had always assumed all of her children would stay within the Amish community—after all, that was how they'd been raised. They'd had a good life. She struggled with being worried about Myra's choices and consciously had to remind herself that there was nothing she could do. *Gott* had given all a gift of free will to choose their own way, and Ettie would have to let Myra choose her own path even though it was one with which Ettie strongly disagreed.

Once Ettie reached the shanty, she put the money in the tin and dialed Ava's number.

After a couple of beeps, a breathless Ava answered. "Hello?"

"Hello, Ava."

"Ettie?"

"Jah, it's me."

"Is everything all right?"

"Jah. We have a visitor here… if you're not on your way out somewhere already, we have a visitor here who would like to see you."

"Who is it?"

"Luc and Genevieve Cohen. She said she would wait until you got here if you want to see the baby."

"Oh, I'd love to see the baby. I was just on my way out to the markets, but I'll do that tomorrow. I'm coming right over now. I've got the buggy ready to go. Bye, Ettie."

Before Ettie could even say goodbye, Ava had hung up the phone in her ear. Ettie walked back to the house still thinking about Myra and how hard it was to let go of someone you once held so tenderly in your arms as a small babe. Myra hadn't written for nearly two years now, and Ettie knew she'd have to face the fact that she might never return to the community.

When Ava arrived at Elsa-May and Ettie's house, she knocked on the door and opened it before anyone had a chance to answer it. Everyone was finishing off the cake in the kitchen when Ava walked in.

"That didn't take long," Elsa-May said.

Ava only had eyes and ears for the baby. She said a brief hello to Mrs. Cohen before she asked if she could hold Luc. Mrs. Cohen handed him over and Ava sat down at the table with them.

"I've missed him," Ava said clutching him to her chest. Ava looked up at them all. "What is the latest?"

Genevieve told her about the boy that could very well be Langley. Ava played along as though she knew nothing. "I do hope he is Langley."

"When Luc grows up, I'll have a wonderful story to tell him about three ladies who looked after him so well when he was a tiny baby."

Ava giggled. "He's made me want to have a baby so bad that I can't tell you."

"And if Langley comes back to us, Luc will have a big brother. It would be too good to hope for. As I said, we're not getting our hopes up, but at the same time, it makes sense that he would be Langley. The detective said that everything fitted with him being Langley. Craig and I are prepared either way. If he's not our boy, at least some other family will be reunited with him."

"That's the best way to look at things," Elsa-May said.

Chapter 22

Late that afternoon, Crowley arrived at Ettie and Elsa-May's house. They hoped he was there to give them an update.

"Have you been helping with the case?" Elsa-May asked.

"No, but I have been keeping up with what's happened. And Kelly said I could let you know that they've picked up George Cousins."

"We heard he was going to be questioned because he was in jail at the same time as Lemonis, and that Kelly was going to check his alibi again."

"He confessed to taking the baby."

"What?" Elsa-May's jaw fell open. "He did?"

"No!" Ettie said. "What about the little boy? Is he Langley?"

"One thing at a time. I'll get to that in a minute. Cousins only confessed when they found photos of Langley on his cell phone. And what's more, there were photos of the baby at different ages. He went on to confess that when he got no money out of the kidnapping, he gave the baby to his sister-in-law. And do you know who his sister-in-law happened to be?"

"No who?" Ettie asked while Elsa-May stared open mouthed.

"A woman called Madeline Davidson, none other than Kel Flower's sister and Nerida Flower's cousin. Madeline's husband died not long before he kidnapped the baby, and the stress of his death caused Madeline to miscarry."

"The Cohen baby is alive?" Elsa-May asked.

"It seems so, as long as it's the same baby. Kelly was trying to keep it quiet, but he had to tell Craig Cohen something when he burst into the station shouting after he'd learned that they'd arrested his wife's secretary. They'll know for certain that he's Langley once they get the DNA results back."

"We had a visit from Genevieve Cohen and she told us about Nerida being arrested."

"I do hope it's Langley," Elsa-May said. "I'd be surprised if it's not, given the circumstances."

Ettie said, "That's the best news we could've hoped for. They were certain their baby had come to a bad end."

"In most kidnapping cases that's what happens. We just have to hope that this one is the exception."

"You'll let us know what happens, won't you?"

"Of course, I will."

* * *

A whole day passed, and Ettie and Elsa-May had heard nothing from anyone. Once it was three o'clock in the afternoon, they just had to contact someone to find out about Langley. Not wanting to disturb the Cohens, they decided to call in on Detective Kelly at the police station.

"We'll get a taxi there and then we should go to the markets and get something for dinner. I think we can do with a night off from cooking."

"We do have some leftovers from last night," Ettie said.

"We can eat that tomorrow for the midday meal.

I feel like something a bit different tonight."

"Before we see Kelly, I need to take that list of names back to Bethany for her to shred. She asked me to do that. It was the only reason she felt comfortable enough to give me the list."

"Okay, we'll do that."

"I don't know why no one has dropped by and told us what's going on. I made that orange cake today because I was certain we'd have visitors and you know how they always like cake. I was certain Kelly or Crowley would stop by."

"Let's go," Elsa-May said. "I'm sure your cake will be eaten."

As they walked down the front steps of their house, Ettie said, "I hope so because I wouldn't have made the cake just for us. I only made it for visitors."

"I hope it's not bad news and that's why we've heard from no one."

"I guess we'll soon find out," Ettie said. "As long as Detective Kelly is at the station and not out somewhere."

Once they'd stopped by Bethany's shop, they proceeded to the police station. They walked up the steps and Elsa-May inquired at the front desk whether Detective Kelly was in. The officer told them Kelly was in and he'd let the detective know they were there.

They sat patiently in the waiting area and Detective Kelly appeared a few minutes later, and beckoned to them.

"He's smiling," Ettie whispered to Elsa-May.

"Jah, that has to be a good sign."

Once they were sitting in his office, Kelly began. "You're here to find out what happened with everything?"

Elsa-May leaned forward. "We're anxious to know about Langley."

"The DNA results came back proving that the little boy in the care of the woman called Madeline Davidson was Langley Cohen."

Elsa-May clapped her hands together. "That's the best news we've ever had."

Ettie felt nothing but relief. "Where is the boy

now?"

"He's back with the Cohens."

"It must be a big adjustment for a four year old to make," Elsa-May said.

"The whole family will be receiving counseling for some time. It's nice to finally have a cold case resolved, and see a family reunited. They're one of the lucky ones."

"I'm so happy for them," Ettie said.

"Well, I've got a ton of paperwork to do. I appreciate how the two of you stayed out of my way on this one."

"Why wouldn't we?" Ettie asked. "It had nothing to do with our community."

"That's true," Detective Kelly said. "I've appreciated your help in the past. The Amish have a way of keeping to themselves."

Elsa-May and Ettie exchanged glances.

"We won't hold you up," Elsa-May said.

As they walked out of the station, Ettie said to Elsa-May, "You know what?"

"What?"

"I should've brought the orange cake for Detective Kelly."

"Why?"

"To eat, of course," Ettie said.

"Weren't you trying to get him to eat better just a few months ago?"

"He could've shared it with the officers. I'm sure they don't get many treats and they work so hard."

"Enough with the dratted cake, Ettie. Stop talking about it."

"Why are you being so irritable? Do you think you might be a diabetic?" Ettie remembered reading somewhere that irritable people might have trouble with their blood sugar levels going up and down.

Elsa-May shook her head. "Let's just get a taxi."

"Weren't we going to the markets?"

"Nee, let's just eat what we've got at home and go to the markets tomorrow."

"Are you tired, Elsa-May?"

"Mm. A little."

That was another sign of diabetes, but Ettie was not brave enough to say any more on that topic. "We should go home past Ava's place and tell her the news."

"*Jah.* She'll be anxious to hear it."

* * *

While Elsa-May dozed off in her chair, Ettie was putting together some leftovers for dinner. Snowy barked and pawed at the door. Ettie walked out of the kitchen to see what the fuss was all about.

"Someone might be here," Elsa-May said pushing herself up to answer the door.

Ettie waited to see if someone was coming while she wiped her hands on a tea towel. It was retired Detective Crowley who was walking to the door.

"I can't sneak up on you anymore with that dog around," he joked.

Elsa-May laughed. "Come inside."

He walked inside and said hello to Ettie. "Have you ladies heard anything?" he asked as he sat down in the living room.

"We hadn't heard from you or anyone else, so we went to the police station this afternoon. We've not long since gotten back home," Ettie said.

Elsa-May continued, "He told us that the baby is Langley. Well, he's not a baby any longer; he's a four year old boy."

"Yes, that's wonderful news. Most botched kidnapping cases have dreadful ends."

"You mentioned that," Elsa-May said. "Perhaps you'd like a slice of orange cake?"

"I'd love some," he said.

Ettie pushed herself up from the couch. "I'll get you a slice and make you a nice cup of hot tea." Ettie returned minutes later with a tray of tea and cake. "I'd already had the pot boiled. I must've known you were coming."

"Now tell me something," Elsa-May said as she leaned forward.

"You're not going to ask him anything about Myra again, are you?" Ettie asked as she poured the tea.

"No, I wasn't. I found out everything I wanted to know about that the other day."

"Good."

"How was that woman able to hide a baby for so long without anyone finding out?"

"She could've kept to herself and maybe she kept on the move," Crowley said. "It was a stroke of luck that you found the connection between the Flowers, Nerida and Kel. I think the people on the case back then might have been distracted by thinking that the first man they arrested—the one they caught collecting the money—knew more than he did. Kel Flower was questioned, but nothing came of it."

"Probably because he wasn't suspected of anything until another case later on, after Langley was taken," Elsa-May said accepting a cup of tea from Ettie.

"That's why the cold case unit has success sometimes. It's often after the crime that things come out in the open—often many years afterward."

"Thank you for helping us, Ronald, you said you would and you did. If it weren't for you, Langley might never have been found."

Crowley laughed. "I don't know about that. The

cold case unit and Kelly would've put the pieces together."

"The thing is, that if Genevieve Cohen had never had another child and left it on our doorstep, and then a man came to take him, there might not have been an investigation with the cold case unit and…"

"And Langley wouldn't have found his way back to his parents. Is that what you were going to say, Ettie?"

"Yes, exactly. You see, it was all meant to be. It's all happened for a reason."

Crowley laughed. "I know what you mean, Ettie. I've solved many cases by synchronistic events and coincidences. I believe someone is watching over us." He picked up a slice of cake.

"Like you baking the orange cake today, Ettie, and now our friend is here to eat it? The orange cake was meant to be." Elsa-May gave a low chuckle.

Ettie frowned at Elsa-May, knowing she was poking fun at her, but she tried not to show it in front of their guest.

"I haven't had orange cake for years and it's my favorite. Only this morning, I was thinking about my late mother and how she used to make an orange cake every Saturday. Did I ever tell you my mother used to make them when I was a child?"

The sisters shook their heads. They knew nothing of his childhood.

He continued, "This orange cake is a sign that things happen for a reason. I know you were joking when you said that to Ettie, Elsa-May, but you don't know how right you were."

Ettie smiled and looked at her older sister and couldn't help feeling a little pleased that Crowley had put her in her place. Elsa-May frowned at her, then tilted her chin and looked away.

"Oh, and I guess I'll need my cell phone back now too," Crowley said. "Unless you ladies would like to hold onto it for a little longer?"

Elsa-May exchanged a smile with Ettie, and Ettie had to suppress a laugh knowing that Elsa-May had the same thought as she. *What would*

Jeremiah have to say about that?

"Thank you for the loan of it, but we'll be sure to give it back to you before you leave," Elsa-May said sweetly.

He took a little child whom he placed among them. Taking the child in his arms, he said to them, "Whoever welcomes one of these little children in my name welcomes me; and whoever welcomes me does not welcome me but the one who sent me."
Mark 9: 36, 37

Thank you for your interest in
Amish Baby Mystery
Ettie Smith Amish Mysteries Book 6

* * * * * * * * * * * * *

For updates on
Samantha Price's new releases,
subscribe to her email list at:
http://www.samanthapriceauthor.com

Other books in this series:

Book 1

<u>Secrets Come Home</u>

After Ettie Smith's friend, Agatha, dies, Ettie is surprised to find that Agatha has left her a house. During building repairs, the body of an Amish man who disappeared forty years earlier is discovered under the floorboards.

When it comes to light that Agatha and the deceased man were once engaged to marry, the police declare Agatha as the murderer. Ettie sets out to prove otherwise.

Soon Ettie hears rumors of stolen diamonds, rival criminal gangs, and a supposed witness to the true murderer's confession. When Ettie discovers a key, she is certain it holds the answers she is looking for. Will the detective listen to Ettie's theories when he sees that the key belongs to a safe deposit box?

Book 2
Amish Murder

When a former Amish woman, Camille Esh, is murdered, the new detective in town is frustrated that no one in the Amish community will speak to him. The detective reluctantly turns to Ettie Smith for help. Soon after Ettie agrees to see what she can find out, the dead woman's brother, Jacob, is arrested for the murder. To prove Jacob's innocence, Ettie delves into the mysterious and secretive life of Camille Esh, and uncovers one secret after another.

Will Ettie be able to find proof that Jacob is innocent, even though the police have DNA evidence against him, and documentation that proves he's guilty?

Can Ettie uncover the real murderer amongst the many people who had reasons to want Camille dead?

Book 3:
Murder in the Amish Bakery

When Ettie has problems with her bread sinking in the middle, she turns to her friend, Ruth Fuller, who owns the largest Bakery in town.

When Ruth and Ettie discover a dead man in Ruth's Bakery with a knife in his back, Ruth is convinced the man was out to steal her bread recipe.

It was known that the victim, Alan Avery, was one of the three men who were desperate to get their hands on Ruth's bread secrets.

When it's revealed that Avery owed money all over town, the local detective believes he was after the large amount of cash that Ruth banks weekly.

Why was Alan Avery found with a Bible clutched in his hand? And what did it have to do with a man who was pushed down a ravine twenty years earlier?

Book 4
Amish Murder Too Close

Elderly Amish woman, Ettie Smith, finds a body outside her house. Everything Ettie thought she knew about the victim is turned upside down when she learns the dead woman was living a secret life. As the dead woman had been wearing an engagement ring worth close to a million dollars, the police must figure out whether this was a robbery gone wrong. When an Amish man falls under suspicion, Ettie has no choice but to find the real killer.

What information about the victim is Detective Kelly keeping from Ettie?

When every suspect appears to have a solid alibi, will Ettie be able to find out who murdered the woman, or will the Amish man be charged over the murder?

Book 5
Amish Quilt Shop Mystery

Amish woman, Bethany Parker, finally realizes her dream of opening her own quilt shop. Yet only days after the grand opening, when she invites Ettie Smith to see her store, they discover the body of a murdered man.

At first Bethany is concerned that the man is strangely familiar to her, but soon she has more pressing worries when she discovers her life is in danger.

Bethany had always been able to rely on her friend, Jabez, but what are his true intentions toward her?

Samantha Price loves to hear from her readers.
Connect with Samantha at:
samanthaprice333@gmail.com
http://twitter.com/AmishRomance
http://www.facebook.com/SamanthaPriceAuthor

Printed in Poland
by Amazon Fulfillment
Poland Sp. z o.o., Wrocław